The
Chosen

By
Verda Foster

ISBN 10: 1-933113-25-1
ISBN 13: 978-1-933113-25-8

CREDITS

EXECUTIVE EDITOR: TARA YOUNG
COVER DESIGN BY DONNA ROBERTS

Published by
Intaglio Publications
P O Box 357474
Gainesville, Florida 32635

Visit us on the web: www.intagliopub.com

DEDICATION

This book is dedicated to my wonderful family. I love you very much.

ACKNOWLEDGMENTS

I would like to once again thank Donna Roberts for another wonderful cover. You rock, Donna.

Thanks also go to Kathy Smith and Tara Young of Intaglio Publications.

This rewritten version of my earlier book, The Chosen, has undergone several changes over the years. I would like to thank my good friend and beta reader Patty Schramm for her insightful feedback. Without a doubt, she helped to make this version of The Chosen a better book.

My sister Vada checked the galley for errors, and her help was very much appreciated.

I would also like to thank Taylor Rickard for suggesting I rewrite this book. Her comments started me on the right path when I started this project.

And lastly, I would like to thank my readers. Without you, there would be no need for books.

Verda Foster
VHFoster@AOL.com

Chapter 1

Roslin sat on the ground with her back against a large oak tree. A cloak was draped around her to protect her from the morning chill. She watched as the first rays of sunlight filtered through the leaves of the trees, overwhelmed by the beauty around her. She had never been allowed away from the palace grounds at home, never basked in the quiet splendor of a forest at sunrise.

Roslin was the only daughter of Lord Athol, the sovereign of Ryshta, and as such, great care had been taken in choosing a suitable husband for her. The wedding was to have taken place when she was seventeen, but when her mother became ill, she begged her father to let her stay by her side through the illness. He had reluctantly consented, and Roslin watched her mother waste away for three years. Now, at twenty, she would finally marry and had been sent to her maternal grandfather, Governor Gage of Frama, so she could meet her betrothed and his family before the wedding.

She remembered her father's words as he sent her off into the unknown. *"Smile and be pleasant, Roslin, and remember it's your duty to please him."*

Reluctantly, she got to her feet and brushed the leaf litter from her dress. She hated to leave, but she needed to get back before she was missed. She pulled the cloak tighter around her shoulders and started down the path that would take her to the carriage that was waiting to carry her home.

The path's gentle slope was easy to traverse, and she walked with a light step until she emerged from the trees and found that her carriage was nowhere to be seen. She frowned and looked around the clearing to make sure this was where she had left her slave waiting. Her cheeks flushed with anger when she realized that she had been deserted.

She let the cloak drop to the ground as she started down the hill, her anger building with every step. *How dare he leave me stranded out here like this!* If she hadn't slipped away without her grandfather's permission, she would go to him and make sure that the insubordinate slave was dealt with appropriately. As it was, she would have to deal with him herself.

Her strides lengthened as she continued toward the city. If she was late for the morning meal, Grandfather Gage would know that she had ventured out of the city unchaperoned. She broke into a run, her breath soon coming in gasps from the unaccustomed exertion.

As she neared her destination, a pain shot through her, and she bent over, clutching at the stitch in her side. Her lungs burned as she tried to take in enough air. When her breathing slowed and the beating of her heart stopped pounding in her ears, she heard shouting coming from the direction of Frama. She cocked her head to listen. Yes, the noise was coming from the city.

The battle was well under way by the time Roslin arrived. She hid herself on the hill overlooking Frama and watched in horror as the fighting below her intensified. Swords flashed and bodies dropped to the ground, and the fighters stepped over the fallen and continued on.

One of the invaders stood out from the rest because he was a head taller than those around him and fought like a man possessed. Roslin watched him slash his way through the soldiers of Frama as if they were children in his path. Finally, she averted her eyes, unable to watch any longer. She could not block out the sounds, though, and listened as the battle raged throughout the day and into the night.

When it was finally over, Roslin slipped from her hiding place and crept into the city. The sounds of wailing women and children filled the night air, and the ground was littered with dead and dying men. She covered her face with her hands and wept, her sobs coming in choking gasps. The sound of something crashing to the ground behind her caused her head to snap up. "They're coming back!" she screamed, and broke into a frantic run toward her grandfather's palace. It would be safe there. Yes, Grandfather would keep her safe.

Roslin's lungs were screaming for air by the time she reached the palace wall. Her hope of a safe haven was shattered when she saw that the invaders had battered down the gates of what she thought was an impenetrable fortress. She took a few moments to catch her breath, then crept closer to the gate and peered into the courtyard.

"Take the wounded men inside to be tended," a voice called out, and Roslin saw it was the tall man she had seen earlier in the day. Men were bustling around to do his bidding, and she reasoned he must be the one in charge. She gasped when she recognized the brand on his arm and backed silently away from the gate. *Slaves. The invaders are slaves.*

A faint voice in the darkness froze her in place. She was almost certain someone had called her name.

"Who is it?" she whispered, but received no reply. The voice was barely audible, but she was sure she heard it. Slowly, she inched her way along the wall, searching the darkness for the source of the sound. She was about to give up when the call came again. Finally, she saw something and moved in that direction. She could now make out the shape of someone on the ground and crept closer to see who had called her name.

"Grandfather," Roslin whispered, as she recognized the battered form below her. Blood seeped from several wounds on his body, and Roslin knelt, pulling him tight against her as tears started down her face again. "There's so much blood," she said. "I don't know what to do."

"There's no hope for me, but there is something you can do. I need you to get out of here as quickly as you can and head for Darius. Your father needs to know what happened here. He needs to be warned."

Roslin shook her head. "I can't leave you here. I'll find someone to help us and we'll both go."

"It's too late for me."

"You're going to be fine," she soothed. "Everything will be fine, you'll see."

"Listen to me, Roslin, I don't have much time. Go now before they find you."

"I can't."

"Stay off the main roads and walk toward the morning sun. Remember that, Roslin, the morning su…" His voice trailed off and his blank eyes stared up at nothing.

"Please don't leave me, Grandfather. I'm afraid."

Roslin rocked him gently back and forth as the tears continued to stream down her face. *Follow the morning sun, Roslin. Follow the morning sun.*

A light rain started to fall an hour into Roslin's journey. She shivered as it began and longed for the cloak that she had so carelessly discarded that morning in the forest above Frama. She knew she had to keep moving. It was the only way to fight the cold.

Roslin forced herself to walk through the night, and at daybreak, she welcomed the sight of a traveler's inn in the distance. She felt an unexpected surge of energy rush through her exhausted body and picked up her pace. Her stomach growled, and she wasn't sure what she needed more—food or sleep.

It dawned on her that the inn would be staffed by slaves, and her pace slowed. Slaves had attacked Frama and could not be trusted anymore. She stopped a moment and studied the structure. The front door stood open, yet not a sound could be heard coming from the building. *Why is it so quiet? Perhaps it's the early hour. Yes, that must be it. No one's up yet.* She stood a moment longer. If no one was awake, why was the door standing open?

Not knowing if they would be friend or foe, Roslin debated whether to approach. Cold and hunger got the best of her, and she decided to risk asking for help. These people could be sleeping, unaware of the carnage that had gone on just a few miles away. She decided to move in cautiously and headed for the side of the building where she could peek in a window.

From this new vantage point, she could see three slave cottages behind and to the side of the inn. Clothes hung on a line in the side yard of one of the cottages, and all the doors were open. *Why would anyone leave their clothes out in the rain overnight? Surely, they would close the door against the night chill.* Something was definitely not right, and Roslin slipped quietly to the window to peer inside.

Nothing stirred, and things were scattered around as if the occupants had made a hasty exit. She went in, and although it was not particularly warm, it was dry. Roslin looked at the cold hearth and desperately wished that she knew how to start a fire.

She had never needed to know such things; someone had always done them for her. She had been raised in the sheltered world of the palace grounds of the sovereign and had never been allowed out to mingle with, or be contaminated by, the slave riffraff, as her father called them. Her slaves were not even allowed to speak to her except to ask how they might serve her.

Roslin searched the inn and found nothing but room after room of empty drawers and cupboards. She moved her search to the cottages in the back and found the same. Her stomach growled, but there would be nothing to eat that night. The missing occupants had taken the entire cache of foodstuffs with them. Exhausted, she curled up on a bare mattress and went to sleep.

It was late afternoon when Roslin woke, feeling more alone then ever. She rolled her stiff and sore body over and pushed herself up on her hands and knees. It seemed to her that there was not a spot on her body that didn't hurt. She walked outside and found the well and pulled up a bucket of water. She drank her fill, then stripped out of her dirt- and blood-encrusted clothes and washed herself in the icy water, wishing again that she knew how to build a fire to heat it.

She shivered as she dashed to the clothesline and pulled off a child's shirt to dry with. She was grateful to have a clean dress to put on and grabbed a large shirt off the line for extra warmth.

She looked at the sky, and her grandfather's words played back in her head: "Follow the morning sun, Roslin."

If I walk toward the morning sun, then I need to walk away from the afternoon sun. Satisfied with her logic, she began to walk again, making sure to keep the sun at her back. She continued her eastward trek long into the night until her feet hurt so badly that she had to stop. She sat to pull her shoes off and gasped when she saw that the skin on her heels and toes had been rubbed away and the area was raw and bleeding. The pain in her feet overshadowed the hunger pains in her empty stomach.

Her feet had never hurt like this before; of course, she had never walked for miles and miles before, either. Anger flooded through her, and she threw her shoes, cursing the murdering slaves who had placed her in this position.

Roslin hugged her legs to her chest, her head dropping to her knees as sobs wracked her body.

The tears finally ended, and she wiped her wet face with the bottom of her shirt and forced herself to get up and start walking again.

It had been four days since Roslin had had anything to eat and three without any measurable amount of water. She discovered that licking the leaves of bushes and the long grasses before the sun evaporated the dew that had settled overnight helped. It was not much, but at least it eased the awful dryness in her mouth. Walking under these conditions was taking its toll, and she found she had to stop frequently. Her belly ached for want of nourishment, and she felt weak and lightheaded. The pain in her feet was constant now, as the bottoms were as raw as the rest, and she cursed herself for leaving her shoes behind. She couldn't stop, though. To stop meant death, and she wasn't ready to give up yet.

Roslin reached the top of a small rise and found she could go no farther. She needed to rest for a while and looked around for a place to sit. Her eyes came to rest on a thicket covered with berries so deep a shade of purple they were almost black. Suddenly, she had the energy to move again, and she stumbled toward the first meal she'd had in days. The berries were sweet but had a bitter tang. The bitter taste did not deter her. To Roslin, they were ambrosia.

After she had eaten her fill, she pulled up the bottom of her shirt to make a pocket to hold more berries. Soon she had stripped the bush of its burden, and her pocket was overflowing. She reasoned that if she was careful and did not overeat like she had just done, the berries would last for three or four days. Feeling pleased with herself, she got her bearings and again started walking. As she reached the bottom of the hill, she felt a cramping in her gut. Within moments, the pain dropped her to her knees in agony. Curling up on the ground, she clutched her stomach and groaned.

As Roslin lay in the dirt wishing she would just die, she heard the sound of many footsteps. She didn't even care if it was the renegade slaves, hoping they would kill her and put her out of her misery.

The group of perhaps twenty men crested the hill and started toward her. Her stomach hurt so much it was hard to focus, but she recognized the tall man she had seen leading the massacre at Frama. He walked to where she was and knelt down, picking up one of the spilled berries.

"Did you eat these?" he asked, holding it up for her to see.

All Roslin could do was nod and groan.

Quickly, he turned her on her side and stuck his fingers down her throat, causing her to gag and retch violently. Then he picked her up and started back up the hill.

"She won't last long without help," he said. "Glen, you're in charge until I get back. Go on ahead and round up the slaves. I'll take her to Mother to tend and join you as soon as I can."

Verda Foster

Chapter 2

Mercifully, Roslin drifted into unconsciousness for the walk back to the invaders' camp and was aware of nothing until she felt firm slaps to her face. She fought to slip back into the black void that took away the pain that had now spread to her head as well as her stomach. The slaps came again, this time harder, and she started awake. She saw an older woman with salt and pepper hair leaning over her.

"I need you to drink this, child," the woman said as she lifted a cup to her lips.

The odor that wafted up was awful, and Roslin pushed it away.

The woman put down the cup and took Roslin's face in her hands. "Listen carefully, child. The berries you ate were poisonous, and I need to purge them from your stomach. This infusion will make sure there's nothing left in your stomach. Do you understand? I'm trying to keep you alive." She reached for the cup again and brought it to Roslin's mouth, and this time, Roslin drank. Almost immediately, the retching started, and the old woman gave her a bucket to use. She heaved until she thought her guts would come out.

When the retching finally ended, the woman again brought a cup to her lips. Roslin no longer had the strength to push it away. "Please…no more," she whispered.

"This one is soothing. It will calm down the cramps in your belly. Sip it slowly, and I promise it'll help."

The warm liquid soothed her throat, and the cramping eased a little. Roslin started to slip into the darkness again when the voice called her back.

"Scoot down so you can hang your legs over the end of the cot, child. I need to take care of these feet."

Roslin screamed when her feet hit the bucket of hot water. She tried desperately to pull them out but didn't have the strength to fight when the old woman held them in place.

"I know the salt water burns, but your feet are infected. This will help."

Tears streamed down Roslin's cheeks, but she stopped fighting. She was grateful when the blackness engulfed her again in its soothing embrace.

The full moon shone brightly in the small clearing at the bottom of the hill. Brice could hear questioning voices drifting his way as his long strides carried him out of the shadows. The response of the slaves, upon casting eyes on him, was always the same—shock, then exuberance that The Chosen had finally come. The prophecy said The Chosen would lead them to freedom. It was said that he would be a giant, with eyes the color of the sacred stone. This had to be him. Six feet tall was rare, and no one had ever seen a man as tall as Brice, whose looming six-feet-four-inch stature dwarfed all those around him.

Brice stepped into the center of the clearing and raised his hands for quiet. A hush fell over the expectant crowd. "My friends, I ask that you move quickly and quietly to your homes and collect your families. Bring them and all the foodstuff you can carry, and my men will lead you to the safety of our camp. At first light, I will lead my army against the Ryshtans of Caiman. Any of you who are willing and able are welcome to join us."

Roslin awoke to find herself lying on a cot in a large tent. Her forehead wrinkled in puzzlement. *How did I get here?* The sun coming through the open door flap told her it was well past midday. She felt ill. Her stomach was sore and her head ached, but the intensity of pain she remembered from the previous day was no longer there. Closing her eyes again, she lay still, her mind trying to pull recent events back into clarity. The last clear memory she had was dropping to the ground with a pain in her belly so great she thought she would die, had in fact wished for death to stop the agony. She tried to sit up, but the room started to spin, and she dropped back down to the cot, closing her eyes and waiting for it to stop. She turned her head to the sound of footsteps and saw a stout woman of middle years with smiling blue eyes and salt and pepper hair walking toward her.

"You made it through the night, child. The worst is over." The woman knelt beside the cot and raised a mug for Roslin to see. "I've brought you some broth." She slipped her free hand under the young woman's shoulders and lifted her a little so she could drink. Roslin gratefully accepted the broth. When the mug was empty, the woman helped Roslin lie back down. "My name is Shea. What do people call you?"

"Roslin."

Shea smiled warmly and patted her hand. "You get some rest, Roslin. I'll be back to check on you a little later."

Roslin watched the woman rise and walk to the tent flap. "How did I get here?" she asked, before Shea could make her exit.

"My son Brice found you and brought you to me to tend," Shea said, turning once again to the young woman. "It's good that he found you when he did; mopoo berries work quickly." With that, she turned and was gone.

As Roslin started to doze off again, a small voice broke through the haze, and she opened her eyes to see the smiling face of a girl perhaps five years old. She was a beautiful child with soft hazel eyes and a mop of auburn curls framing her sweet face.

The girl reached out to touch her cheek. "When I don't feel good, my papa tells me a story. Would you like me to tell you a story?"

Roslin really didn't feel like staying awake to listen to the girl. "Perhaps later," she said.

The smile disappeared from the elfin face, and the little girl turned to go.

"Wait, I've changed my mind," Roslin said, patting the edge of the cot. "I think perhaps you're right. A story might make me feel better."

The girl quickly climbed up and sat down, the smile returning to her face. She straightened Roslin's covers and tucked them in around her.

"Thank you for taking care of me," Roslin said. "What's your name?"

"Cadie."

The girl's imagination kicked in then, and Roslin listened as Cadie spun her tale. She liked the child. There was something familiar about her, but she couldn't place it. When the story ended, Cadie looked at her expectantly. "Thank you, Cadie, I do feel a little better."

The girl grinned from ear to ear. "Do you want me to tell you another?"

"I would love one later, Cadie, but right now I think I need to sleep." She patted the girl's hand.

Cadie nodded and reached over and felt Roslin's forehead and cheek the way she had seen her grandmother do for Roslin while she slept. She didn't know why Gram had done it, but it made her feel important to pretend she did. It felt good to know that she had been able to make the lady feel better. "I'll take good care of you," she said, as she climbed down from the cot.

"I know you will." The girl was so cute that Roslin had to smile. She watched Cadie leave, and she realized what was familiar about the child. Her smile was so much like her younger brother Kyle's. It was more than that, something in the eyes, too. She drifted off to sleep with a smile on her face, thinking about the sweet child.

When Roslin awoke again in the early evening, her bladder told her it was time to be emptied. She sat up and noted that the dizziness had eased along with the headache. She felt weak and shaky but otherwise much better. She swung her legs over the edge of the cot and noticed for the first time that her feet were bandaged. She let them touch the ground and was relieved to find that although they still hurt, the padding on her feet helped. Slowly and painfully, she made her way to the door and turned to walk toward the privacy of the brush surrounding the campsite.

As Roslin returned to the clearing, she heard the sound of many horses. She looked in the direction of the sound and was horrified to see a large group of men riding into camp led by the same tall man she had seen at Frama. He had blood spattered all over him, and she wondered how many innocent lives he had taken today. He lifted his sword, and she heard him shout, "Caiman has been liberated." The cheer that sounded around her was deafening, and she covered her ears. Panic gripped her when she realized that she was in the camp of the slaves who had attacked Frama and killed her grandfather. She felt a hand on her shoulder and shrank away from it.

"It's all right, child," Shea said. "We won. No harm will come to you." She smiled. "Let's get you back to bed. I'm going to have my hands full with our wounded; I don't need to be worrying about you, too."

Roslin allowed herself to be led back into the tent and put to bed. For some reason, these people believed her to be one of them, which explained why they were so kind to her. She was grateful that Shea had not tried to bathe her or it would have been obvious that she was Ryshtan. Her skin was unblemished by the brand that all slaves carried. Her father had explained to her long ago that the brand was to prevent a slave from running away and pretending to be a free man in another city. All strangers entering any city in Ryshta had to have their arm inspected for the brand.

As Roslin lay on the cot, she wondered at her fate. She had to let these renegades believe she was one of them, lest she suffer the same fate as Grandfather Gage. When her feet were healed and she was stronger, she would try to escape; but for now, she had no choice but to stay and hope that her true identity was not discovered. A sweet little voice brought her out of her musings.

"I brought you some thick soup and bread," Cadie said, holding a bowl out to her new friend.

Roslin looked over to see the girl with a bowl in one hand and a hunk of bread in the other. She sat up and accepted the food. "Thank you," she said, smiling at the child.

Cadie sat beside Roslin and watched her eat. "My papa says that someday we will all live in real houses and not have to travel around fighting like this anymore."

Roslin turned to the child and asked, "Would you like that, Cadie?"

"Oh, yes! Papa said we'll have a flower garden because my mama loved them so."

"What happened to your mama?"

"Papa says she died when I was just a babe. I don't remember her, but I know all about her. My papa tells me about her all the time. He said she was beautiful and she loved me very much."

Roslin felt sorry for this little girl, losing her mother and being raised by this traveling army of barbarians. "I'm sure she loved you, and I'll bet you grow up to be just as beautiful as she was."

The two of them spent the rest of the evening talking, and Roslin let Cadie tell her another story. The girl was so open and friendly Roslin couldn't help but like her.

The wounded had finally all been seen to, and Brice sat by the fire to relax and get a bite to eat before retiring for the night. He had cleaned the blood off his body and finally felt human again. It had been a long day, and he was tired. As he ate, he thought back over the day and was grateful that his casualties had been few. They would stay here a few days to give the wounded a chance to rest, then move toward their final destination. He needed his army well rested and in top shape to defeat the sovereign.

Darius, the capital of Ryshta, was the largest of the fifteen city-states and was by far the best armed. Brice had saved Darius for last, letting his army grow with each city he liberated. Now he was ready to face the sovereign with a force that he believed could win.

They had started at the farthest edge of Ryshta and worked their way toward the capital. It had been a hard-fought campaign, but with the army growing steadily with each conquest, each victory was easier than the last. In just a few short months, they had done what the elders back home in Darius had said was impossible. The final victory was in sight, and he could taste it.

Standing and stretching, Brice made his way toward the tent he shared with his family. As he approached, he heard the sounds of laughter and talking and stopped to listen. His daughter Cadie was talking to the silly woman who tried to kill herself with mopoo berries. Apparently, she was feeling much better. It was such a joy to hear the happy sounds after a day like today. He could hear that Cadie was telling one of her stories and receiving much praise from the stranger. He decided he liked this woman who was taking such pains to be kind to his daughter.

Brice lifted the tent flap and walked inside. Cadie was sitting on the woman's lap, and the woman had the most radiant smile on her face. *She really is beautiful,* he thought to himself. She had long golden hair, and her eyes were a pale yellow green. The only time he had really looked at the woman, her face had been so twisted in pain that he hadn't noticed her beauty at all.

"Papa!" Cadie shouted, running to him and throwing herself into his arms.

"Mmm, you give the best hugs," Brice said, as her small arms wrapped around his neck and squeezed tightly. He kissed the top of her head, then looked to the woman. "I'm Brice," he said, extending his hand to her. "Thank you for being so kind to my daughter."

Roslin took his hand. Up close, it was hard to imagine this smiling man capable of the carnage she had witnessed at Frama. She had never seen a man so tall, so pleasing to the eye before; he truly was beautiful.

"My name's Roslin, and it was my pleasure. You have a charming little girl; I enjoyed spending time with her. She's been taking good care of me." She smiled at the beaming child. "I really should be the one thanking you. I'm told you're the one who saved my life," Roslin continued, totally drawn into those incredible blue eyes. She had never felt this strong an attraction toward anyone, and the fact that it was directed at the leader of the rebel slaves startled her.

Repeating the young woman's sentiments, Brice said, "The pleasure was all mine." Roslin's smile was captivating, and he couldn't help smiling back. Still holding her hand, Brice lifted it to his lips, gently kissing her knuckles.

The tent flap opened, and Shea stepped inside. "We've finished tending to the injured and settled them down for the night," she said. She reached to take Cadie out of Brice's arms. "Morning comes early, little one. I think it's time you went to bed."

"Please tell me a story before I go to sleep," Cadie begged, hugging her father's neck tightly.

Shea noticed a rip in the back of Brice's shirt and the red torn skin beneath. She shook her head. "You'll have to get your story tomorrow night, Cadie. I need to get your papa's wounds dressed." She ushered the child to her cot and put her to bed.

"I'm all right, Mother, it's just a scratch."

"Scratch or not, it needs to be cleaned and dressed." She led Brice around the privacy screen that separated his sleeping area from the rest of the tent. "Now get that shirt off so I can take a look at you."

"Yes, ma'am," he said, pulling the shirt gingerly over his head to display a shallow gash about two inches long on his lower back, just above his waist.

"It doesn't look too bad," Shea admitted, as she cleaned and dressed the wound.

"I told you it was only a scratch."

"I'm a mother," Shea said. "I have a right to pamper my babies."

Brice pulled a nightshirt over his head, then pulled her into his arms. "I love you," he said, and kissed the top of her head. He heard her sigh and backed away to get a better look at her. "Are you all right, Mother?"

"I'm fine," Shea said, patting Brice's face. "Just tired, I guess."

Brice took her hands between his and squeezed gently. "We'll be staying here for a few days. You'll be able to get some rest. Now go on to bed, I'm fine. Thank you." He watched Shea leave, then lay down, his thoughts drifting to the beautiful young woman on the other side of the tent.

Roslin also lay awake, unable to stop thinking about Brice and her unexpected attraction to him. It was hard to reconcile this man, whose eyes shone with such love when he looked at Cadie, with the memories she had of the devastation at Frama.

Chapter 3

Morning found Brice still thinking about the beautiful young woman recovering in his tent. He hadn't felt this kind of attraction for anyone since Elsbeth, and he couldn't push away the feeling that he was being disloyal to his lost love. The night before, the attraction had been so strong, but now in the light of day, he could see things more clearly. Roslin was just another woman in camp. No more, no less. He had no reason to feel guilty.

Shea was sitting by the fire when Brice emerged from the tent.

"Do you want to tell me about it?" Shea asked as she handed him a steaming cup.

"What?" Brice answered, puzzled at the question.

"I know something is troubling you. Please...let me help." Shea patted the empty spot on the log beside her.

Brice looked around the campsite. It was early, they were alone, and he did need someone to talk to. Accepting the proffered cup, he sat, staring into the fire. "It's silly, really." Brice looked into his mother's concerned eyes. "I find myself drawn to Roslin, and it scares me."

"Because of what happened with Elsbeth?"

Brice nodded, his gaze returning to the fire. "I hardly know the woman, yet I feel drawn to her, and I got the feeling last night that she was attracted to me, as well." Brice put down his cup and took her hands into his own. "I loved Elsbeth, Mother, and I lost her because of what I am. I don't know if I could go through that again."

Shea lifted her hands and cupped Brice's face. "So you think it's better to live a life of loneliness? To never allow yourself to love or be loved?"

"No, of course not. But this is different."

"Why is it different?"

Brice looked back into the fire. "I don't know, it just is. I feel disloyal."

Shea bristled at those words. "Listen to me, Brice. If there's one thing you're not, it's disloyal. I watched you put up that wall when she left you, and it broke my heart. Five years is long enough to mourn. If someone has come along that might reach into your heart again, you should give yourself permission to get to know her without feeling disloyal. Just enjoy getting to know her and don't rush things. You have plenty of time."

Brice smiled. "You always seem to know what to say."

"I'm your mother, and I love you."

Brice wrapped his arms around Shea, pulling her close. "I love you, too."

Camp was starting to come alive as people began their morning chores. Brice saw Roslin and Cadie leave the tent and watched Roslin as she slowly limped into the tall brush for her morning visit. He wondered how many miles she had walked to do that kind of damage to her feet. Brice hurried to the edge of the brush and waited for Roslin to emerge. When she did, he picked her up to carry her back to the tent. "You need to keep off these feet as much as possible for a few days," he said. "If I'm around, you just call me and I'll carry you." He smiled shyly at her and started for the tent.

Roslin was a little flustered at being held in the strong arms of the man to whom she found herself very attracted. "I don't want to be a burden," she answered, a shy smile creeping onto her face, as well. Her heart had started beating wildly, and she wondered again at being attracted to a man she considered a barbarian. But she was, and she couldn't help herself.

"Believe me, you're no burden," Brice said, as he placed Roslin gently on her cot. "I haven't eaten yet. Can I bring you something and share the morning meal with you?"

Roslin smiled again. "That would be nice, thank you."

Returning the smile, Brice turned and left the tent, leaving a very confused young woman behind.

Roslin smiled when she thought about how wonderful it had felt to be in Brice's arms. She had watched him with Cadie. He was so loving and gentle with her that she could almost forget that he or one of his men had murdered her grandfather. The smile faded as the reality of the situation set in. *What are you doing?* she asked herself, and pushed back the attraction she was feeling for Brice.

She thought of him as she saw him that night— terrifying, with his bloody sword slashing through bodies. *He destroyed Frama.* When Brice was not near, she could think clearly. She excused her behavior by reminding herself that she had to be nice to him until she could make her escape. If Brice found out who she was, he would surely kill her.

Brice returned with two hearty bowls of porridge, accompanied by Cadie, who carried a bowl of her own.

"We came in here to eat with you," the child said, as she sat on the cot beside Roslin.

Cadie always seemed to have a smile on her face, and Roslin couldn't help but respond to it. "I can't think of anyone I would rather share a meal with," she said, grinning back at the child.

Brice smiled as he watched Roslin and Cadie chat while they ate. It was clear that his daughter found Roslin as appealing as he did. That was good. He could not imagine letting an attraction, no matter how strong it was, go beyond that if Cadie did not like her.

The sounds of children playing outside the tent caught Cadie's attention, and she ran to the door to see what the game was about. "Can I play, too?" she called, as she dashed out the door, forgetting her half-eaten porridge.

Brice was both relieved and annoyed at the quick departure. He wanted to be alone with Roslin but found himself tongue tied and couldn't think of anything to say. At least Cadie had kept the conversation going. "My mother tells me you have no memory of my finding you and bringing you here," he finally said, after a few silent moments.

"No, none at all."

"Perhaps it's for the best. You were very sick."

"Yes, I guess some things are best forgotten." Roslin thought back to Frama and wished those images could be erased from her mind. Brice was so different here with his family, and he had been so kind to her. She decided to push the image of the other Brice back and hold on to the Brice who seemed to care for her.

"When I found you, it looked like you had been walking for days. Where had you come from?" Brice asked, thinking again of the young woman's feet.

Roslin thought quickly and decided to avoid talking about her past by simply pretending not to remember anything before waking in Brice's tent. Shea had already confirmed that she had no memory of him finding her, and this way, she would not have to come up with a story to remember correctly or worry about getting caught in a lie. "I…I can't remember anything before you brought me here." Roslin looked away, afraid he would see the lie in her eyes.

"Don't worry, I'm sure it'll come back to you," Brice said, trying to reassure her. "And remember, if your past doesn't come back to you, you still have a lifetime ahead of you to build new memories that I hope I can be a part of."

Roslin looked up into sincere blue eyes and melted. She couldn't believe what his gaze did to her. "I hope so, too," she said, smiling shyly

Brice decided it was time to again distance himself from Roslin. He had been desperately lonely for so long that now that he was giving himself permission to care for someone, his body was pushing him to move too fast. He could feel it happening and was helpless to stop it.

"I need to check on my men and see how the wounded are faring," he said, taking Roslin's hand and kissing it. Brice picked up the bowls and started to leave. "I'll check back on you later. If you need to go somewhere before I return, send Cadie to fetch me." He smiled down at the young woman, then turned and left.

Brice walked through the large camp toward the area that had been set up for the wounded. He made the rounds, giving praise for a job well done and encouragement to those with serious injuries. The rebel leader tried to keep his mind on what he was doing, but his thoughts kept returning to the woman recovering in his tent. Without even realizing where he was walking, Brice found himself staring at the footprints Roslin had left at the edge of camp that morning as she entered the shelter of the brush to relieve herself. He knelt and touched the print just as a fine rain started to fall. He thought again about Roslin's feet and decided she needed protection for them as they healed. Quickly, he measured the footprints, knowing that they would soon disappear into the wet ground.

The rain started coming down in earnest, and the camp was suddenly alive with people scurrying to shelter. Brice walked to one of the covered supply wagons and climbed inside. Rummaging around, he found some scraps of leather and leather cord. *This will do nicely*, he thought, a smile spreading across his face. It was not enough leather for a proper pair of shoes but would be plenty to make a pair of sandals.

Roslin's feet would be too tender for some time for regular shoes, and sandals would give her the protection she needed to heal. It had been a long time since Brice had taken the time to sit with his leather tools and work, and he found it relaxing. His mind kept returning to the woman who would wear the sandals. How would Roslin react when she learned his secret? He shook his head. Better not to dwell on that.

When Brice finished, he inspected his handiwork one more time before he started off toward his tent to check the fit and to see if Roslin approved. Exiting the wagon, he was relieved to see the rain had stopped and the ground had already started to dry out. He glanced at the sun and noted that it was almost straight up in the sky. Brice marveled that he had been so engrossed in his work that he hadn't even noticed the passage of time.

Brice entered the tent and found that Cadie was again entertaining their houseguest. He walked over and knelt in front of Roslin. "I made these for you. Shall we see if they fit?" Brice lifted each bandaged foot and slipped the shoes on, tying them securely.

Roslin was overwhelmed by the gesture. "They're perfect. Thank you." She felt a warm flush and looked away, needing to distance herself from those eyes that seemed to be calling to her. "Now I won't need to impose on you to carry me around."

"I don't mind. How could I object to having such a beautiful woman in my arms?"

Roslin's blush deepened. *He's flirting with me again.* "Well then, perhaps you wouldn't object to carrying me out one more time for a little visit with the bushes before bedtime."

Brice smiled and scooped Roslin into his arms. "I wouldn't object at all." Any excuse to hold Roslin was welcome. He carried her to the edge of the clearing and set her down but kept his arms around her. It had been so long since he had held a woman in his arms, and his body was reacting to the feel. His heart started to pound, and he wished he could make love to her right here and now. He leaned down and kissed her gently on the lips, pleased that Roslin did not seem to object. When he pulled her closer and tried to deepen the kiss, he felt her tense and immediately pulled away. "I'm sorry...I..."

Roslin placed her fingers to Brice's lips to silence him. "Shh, it's all right...I wanted you to...but I think we need to slow this down. It's happening too fast." She paused a moment to gather her thoughts. "I need to know that there's more between us than just a physical attraction. I want the passion I feel when I'm in your arms, but I need more than that."

Roslin searched the blue depths of the rebel leader's eyes, hoping her words would not drive him away. The gaze was warm and accepting, and it gave her the courage to go on. "I want to savor every moment when I make love for the first time and know that the one I love returns those feelings. I hope you can understand."

Brice kissed the fingers that still rested against his lips and smiled. "I understand, and there's no hurry. We'll take all the time we need."

"Thank you."

When they returned to the tent, Shea was pulling a nightshirt over Cadie's head. She patted her behind and said, "Off to bed with you now, little one."

Cadie looked over to Brice pleadingly. "Did you forget, Papa? You promised to tell me a story tonight."

"I guess I did, didn't I? All right, but just one." He picked her up and placed her on her cot and pulled the blanket over her. "What would you like to hear?"

"Tell me again how you and my mama first knew you loved each other," Cadie answered, stifling a yawn.

"All right. Close your eyes and I'll tell you all about it." Tired eyes closed, and as Brice began to speak, he brushed a wayward lock of auburn hair from Cadie's face. Try as she might, the child could not stay awake, and soon Brice heard the gentle, even breathing of sleep. He leaned down and kissed her forehead. "I won't ever let her forget you, Elsbeth," he whispered, as his mind drifted back again to that time so long ago.

Brice sat keeping watch over the lovely sorrel mare Sabiea. She was due to drop her foal at any time. Her first foal had been found dead the morning after its birth, and they were not sure if it had been stillborn or if the mare's inexperience had simply caused her to leave it to suffocate. Brice was taking no chances with this foal and intended to keep watch until it made its appearance. He glanced over to the sleeping figure of his friend Elsbeth and smiled. They had been friends for years, but of late, Brice found he could not look at her without his heart starting to race and warmth spreading through his body. They had agreed to take turns with the watch, but the girl looked so peaceful that Brice did not have the heart to waken her. Her hair was of the deepest auburn and framed her face in soft curls. As the young trainer watched, soft gray-green eyes fluttered open, and Elsbeth stretched and sat up. Yawning, the girl crawled out of her pallet in the straw and joined Brice on the bench against the barn wall.

"Did you forget to wake me?" she asked, smiling at her friend.

"I wasn't tired, so I thought I'd let you sleep a while longer." Brice turned away from the girl, not wanting her to see the flush he could feel spreading across his face and neck.

Elsbeth saw the blush and smiled. Finally, a sign, *she thought. She had had a crush on Brice for some time now and decided if he was too shy to declare his feelings for her, she would have to be the one to make the first move. She leaned over and sweetly kissed the flushed cheek. "I love you, Brice," she said, as she felt redness color her cheeks, as well.*

"I...I love you, too," Brice stammered, as he tried to will his heart to stop pounding its way out of his chest.

Elsbeth smiled. "Come...put your head in my lap and get some sleep." She saw the hesitant look in the young trainer's eyes. "You don't have to worry, I'll keep watch," she said, patting her lap. "Come on."

Brice scooted down the bench and lay down, looking up into gray-green eyes.

"Now close your eyes," Elsbeth instructed, running her fingers through Brice's thick dark hair. She began to hum softly, and soon the exhausted young trainer was sound asleep.

The second night of their watch found the young couple hoping the mare would take her time and not be in any hurry to drop this foal. Brice made a nest of straw against the wall, and they spent the early part of the night talking and cuddling, neither wanting to sleep but knowing they had to.

"It's your turn to sleep," Brice said, his fingers lightly stroking up and down the young woman's arm. "I love touching you." He leaned over to kiss her cheek.

Elsbeth reached up and encircled Brice's neck and held him as she turned and offered her lips instead of her cheek. She had longed to feel Brice's lips against hers, and she intended to make sure it happened.

Brice could not turn down such an invitation. He thought his heart would stop when he felt the softness of Elsbeth's lips caressing his own. Again and again they kissed, not caring if they ever slept again.

"What do you think you're doing?" Eamon shouted, pulling Brice off his young friend.

"We were just kissing, Father...I swear."

"You're too young for this kind of foolishness."

"I'm sixteen, Father."

Eamon looked at Elsbeth. "And how old are you, girl?"

"Fifteen, sir."

"You're both just babies." He raised his hand as if to strike Brice.

Elsbeth grabbed his arm. *"Please, sir, we didn't do anything wrong...we just kissed."* Tears started down her cheek. *"I love Brice."*

Eamon lowered his arm and looked at her sadly. *"Go home, girl. I'll keep watch with Brice."*

She looked at Brice, the fear plain on her face that if she left, his father might strike him.

"Go on home," Brice said, wiping the tears from Elsbeth's face. *"I'll be all right."* He watched until she was gone before turning to Eamon.

"I love her," he said, trying to hold back the tears he felt at the disappointment he saw in his father's eyes.

"And just what do you expect to tell her when she wants more than you can give? She will find out the truth. What then?" He closed his eyes and slowly shook his head. Putting a hand on each of Brice's shoulders, he asked. *"What if she wants children? Have you thought of that?"*

"She loves me She'll understand."

"Will she?"

They heard a grunt from the stall and realized that the mare was in hard labor. *"We'll talk more of this another time,"* Eamon said, then turned and walked toward the stall.

Brice tucked the covers tightly around Cadie, then stood and walked to Roslin's cot and squatted in front of her.

"I have the early watch tonight, so I must take my leave." He lifted Roslin's hand and kissed it. "Good night."

Roslin watched him go and knew she had a silly grin on her face. She also felt an unexpected fluttering in her stomach. *Is this what it feels like to be falling in love?* It felt good, and that was all she cared about. She closed her eyes and pictured Brice holding her in his arms and kissing her. A shiver ran through her body that was not at all unpleasant. She was brought out of her daydreaming when she felt Shea sit beside her on the cot.

"Brice seems to be very taken with you, child. I haven't seen him behave this way toward a woman since Elsbeth." She patted Roslin's hand. "Be gentle with his heart; it's taken so long to mend. I would hate to see it shattered again. When he lost Elsbeth, it changed him. The only thing he lived for was to one day free our people from the Ryshtans. It's been almost five years, and this is the first time he has let anyone get close. It would break my heart if he shut off his emotions again."

Roslin shuddered at the thought of what might happen if Brice found out that she was Ryshtan. "I care very much for Brice. I would never purposefully hurt him."

"I'm sure you wouldn't. I just want you to be aware of the power you hold. Don't let him push too fast. A starving man will sometimes destroy himself when a banquet is placed before him. The body is not the only part of us that can starve. Hearts can starve, too, and Brice's heart has been starving for some time now." Shea smiled. "Well, I think I need to get these old bones to bed. Morning comes early." Rising, she walked to her cot and prepared for sleep.

Roslin lay back and let her mind wander again over the events of the day. How could she be attracted to someone one day and believe she was falling in love the next? Could things like this really happen that fast? She was glad they had had the talk about slowing things down; she needed to be sure of her feelings before she could commit to a relationship, and she wanted him to be sure, too, especially now after talking to Shea.

Verda Foster

Chapter 4

Shea was off somewhere, and Roslin and Cadie had been left to entertain each other. Cadie provided an endless stream of chatter, and Roslin had to laugh at her vivid imagination.

She was laughing loudly when Brice came in and scooped her up in his arms.

"I think it's time for you to meet more of my family," he said, as he carried Roslin out the door and started for the other side of camp.

"My feet are feeling much better today; you really don't need to carry me. I can walk," Roslin said, even though she was enjoying being in his arms again.

"It's a long walk," Brice answered. "Humor me."

Roslin nodded and smiled. She almost wished her feet were not healing so well. It would not be long before Brice would have no excuse to carry her about. They reached their destination, and Roslin saw Shea and another woman sitting and talking together. Two children several years older than Cadie came running over to greet them, and Brice put Roslin down.

"These are my brother Glen's sons." Brice placed a hand on the older boys shoulder, "This is Bowen, and this is Tully." He ruffled the fine red hair on the younger boy's head.

Roslin smiled, shaking first Bowen's hand, then his brother's. "I'm very pleased to meet you." The woman who had been talking with Shea came forward, extending her hand. "I'm Lessa, Glen's wife. I see you've met my boys." She took Roslin's hand and pulled her toward the fire. "Why don't you get off your feet and I'll get you something to eat?"

"Thank you," Roslin answered, as she followed the friendly woman to a log by the fire.

Brice walked over and sat by her side while Shea and Lessa began dishing up plates of food. "Where's Glen?" he asked Lessa when she handed him a plate.

"He went to feed the horses. I expect he'll be back soon."

A pleasant-looking man approached their group and smiled down at the blonde woman sitting next to Brice. "You must be Roslin. I'm Glen. Brice has told me all about you. I'm glad to see you're feeling better." Lessa brought him a plate and he winked at her. "Thank you, love."

"Much better," Roslin answered, "thank you for your concern."

Roslin studied the man. His hair was dark brown like Brice's, but other than that, she could see no resemblance between the brothers. His eyes were a soft brown, and his nose was larger with a little bump, where Brice's was straight.

"Mother tells me you have no memory before coming to our camp. That must be most distressing."

Roslin's eyes fell to her lap. She hated lying and found she could not look Glen in the eye when she did. "Yes, most distressing."

Brice could see Roslin's discomfort and squeezed her hand. "This is good," he said to Lessa, trying to change the subject. "It's a wonder what you can do with trail rations."

"Yes, it's very good," Roslin agreed, the smile returning to her face. She found that she liked these people very much. They didn't have much, but what they had, they shared. They seemed to truly care for one another, and despite the hard life they were living, they seemed happy. She tried to think back to a time in her life when she could say the same and failed. She shuddered at the thought of ever going back to that kind of existence.

Brice climbed to the top of the small rise that overlooked camp. It was almost sunset, and it felt good to just sit and relax. His wounded men were on the mend, and in a few more days, they could start moving again.

He closed his eyes and let his mind dream of a time when all this fighting would be behind him and he and his family could settle into a permanent home. The sound of footsteps brought him out of his daydream, and he opened his eyes to see Roslin walking toward him on the path.

"May I join you?" she asked.

"Please do." Brice smiled and patted the ground beside him.

Roslin sat and tucked her legs underneath her. "You looked so lost in thought that I wasn't sure if I should disturb you."

"I was just imagining what it'll be like when this is over and I never have to fight again."

"Can't you end it now?"

Brice shook his head. "As long as Lord Athol is in power, it can never be over."

"You could talk to him. Reach some kind of agreement."

"You can't reason with people like him, Roslin."

"How can you know unless you try?"

"I grew up in Darius," Brice said. "I've had many encounters with Lord Athol, so you can believe me when I say I know. The man's pure evil, and he has to be stopped."

"I didn't know you were from Darius."

Brice smiled and lay down and laced his fingers behind his neck. "I bred and trained the sovereign's horses. I was his master trainer."

"His master trainer?" Roslin said. "My, you must have been very good at it."

"I worked with my father from the time I was seven. I loved working with the horses. I hope to do it again one day."

Roslin smiled. "They're such beautiful creatures; I'd love to learn to ride."

"Then learn you shall," Brice said. "We'll begin tomorrow."

Roslin reached to pat the jaw of the large gray mare, but the horse's head turned toward her, and she quickly pulled her hand back.

"You don't need to be afraid," Brice said. "She's quite gentle."

"She looked at me."

"She just wanted to see who you were." Brice grabbed Roslin's hand and placed it on the mare's neck. "Her name is Night Wind."

Fear showed plainly in Roslin's eyes, but she kept her hand where Brice placed it. "She's beautiful."

Brice handed Roslin the horse's reins. "I think today we'll just let you get to know her." He stepped away and Roslin froze, her eyes wide with fright. "Walk," he instructed. "She'll follow."

Roslin didn't move, and Brice stepped closer and retrieved the reins. "Are you sure you want to learn to ride?"

"I do." Roslin glanced at the large animal standing beside her. "It's just that I've never been this close to a horse before."

"Never?"

Roslin shook her head.

Brice handed her the reins again but did not step away. "We'll walk her together. Is that okay?"

Roslin nodded and Brice stepped beside her and took her arm. They started to walk, and the large animal fell in step beside them. After a few minutes, Roslin began to relax and enjoy herself. Soon the big mare lipped the side of her cheek and ear, and Roslin giggled at the tickle. She patted Night Wind's jaw and smiled. "I think she likes me."

As the days passed, Brice spent every moment he could spare with Roslin, and their closeness continued to grow. His one fear was that when he told Roslin the truth about himself, she wouldn't want him. He prayed that this time it would be different. That once he had Roslin's heart, nothing else would matter.

For now he would be content with snatches of time between the work required to make sure everything was ready for the battle with the sovereign. This battle was the culmination of years of work, and with the defeat of Darius, the last of his people would finally be free.

The days flew by too quickly. Their brief respite was over, and it was time to start for Darius again. Any of the wounded who were still not up to sitting astride a horse were loaded into wagons. The last leg of the journey had begun, and Brice was anxious to put this part of his life behind him and hopefully begin a new one with Roslin.

Mounting his horse, Brice rode to where Roslin was waiting her turn to climb into the wagon with Shea and Cadie. "Ride with me?" he asked, extending his hand.

Roslin smiled and accepted the hand. She wrapped her arms around Brice and snuggled close, laying her head against his strong back. *What is it about Brice that captivates me so?* He was not like any man she had ever met. There was something different about him that she couldn't quite identify. Whatever it was, it drew her to him, and she realized she had totally lost her heart to the man.

They walked to the beginning of the procession and cantered ahead, leaving the slow-moving caravan behind. Alone with Roslin, Brice sighed at the feel of the young woman pressed so closely against him.

They were five days into the trip, and anticipation built steadily as they got closer to Darius. This was it. The final battle in a hard-won fight for freedom. Brice and Roslin rode ahead as usual and were just returning to check on the progress of the caravan when the sound of loud voices could be heard.

The rebel leader saw a group of men gathered around a large wagon, while others were glancing down an embankment at the edge of the road. Brice urged his horse closer and dismounted, walking to the edge to see what was causing the stir. He could see one of the supply wagons at the bottom about twenty feet down. It was broken into several pieces, and supplies were scattered everywhere.

"What happened?" he asked, turning his gaze to Glen, who was striding his way.

"We broke an axle on our wagon, and that damn fool Trustin tried to go around us and went over the edge.

"He jumped clear, but the wagon isn't salvageable."

Brice was angry and frustrated at the delay. There were still several hours of daylight left, and to lose them meant that the battle would have to be put off a day. He had hoped to arrive just outside Darius early the next evening. They would then send a few men to spread the word through the slave village that The Chosen had arrived. They would be warned that there would be a battle at first light and they should take their families and flee to the woods until it was safe.

Brice turned back to Glen. "How long to fix it?"

"Four or five hours. We don't have a replacement. I'll have to make one."

Brice shook his head. There was nothing to be done about it now.

"Okay, there's a clearing about two hundred yards ahead. We'll set up camp there." Brice looked at the men standing around the crippled wagon. "Some of you men get this wagon moved over to let the rest pass safely."

Camp was set up quickly, and Glen started to work on repairing the broken axle, while others made a living chain to pass the scattered supplies hand to hand up the slope. Roslin watched Brice pace back and forth. It was obvious he was upset, and she decided to try to take his mind off the problems that vexed him so. Walking over, she took his hand. "Come…walk with me."

Brice squeezed her hand. "I'd like that." He decided it was time to tell Roslin his secret. She deserved to know the truth.

They walked to a stand of trees not far from camp and stopped out of the sight of prying eyes. Brice took her face in his hands and spoke, his voice trembling.

"You take my breath away." He leaned down and kissed Roslin and was surprised when she opened her mouth and hesitantly touched his lips with her tongue. He deepened the kiss, his heart pounding when Roslin moaned into his mouth. "I love you," Brice whispered. "But before we take this any further, there's something important about me you need to know." He let his hands slide up Roslin's arms.

Roslin felt Brice's hands slipping under her sleeves, caressing her arms, and panicked. If he continued, he was sure to discover she had no brand. She pushed Brice away and hastily pulled her sleeve back down to cover her bare arm. She watched Brice's face change from passion to puzzlement.

Brice saw the panic in Roslin's face, and his heart sank. *She couldn't think I would force myself on her, could she?* Then it registered. Why was Roslin so desperate to cover her arm? He remembered the smoothness of her skin. It was too smooth; there was no brand. And the way Roslin reacted, she was very aware of that fact. There had been no memory loss...she had lied. Brice reached for her arm again, and Roslin froze as her sleeve was pushed up to reveal a blemish-free arm.

"You lied to me," Brice said, closing his eyes with sad acceptance.

"No," Roslin said. "You have to believe me. I really didn't remember you finding me and taking me to your camp. You all assumed I was one of you, and I didn't volunteer the truth."

"I took you into my family, took care of you. I thought we were becoming... Why didn't you tell me?"

Roslin remembered the other Brice...the one she had seen in the heat of battle...the Brice who didn't seem real anymore. She had to make him understand the terror she felt when she first found herself sheltered under that Brice's tent. She had a very real fear of being killed if he found out she was Ryshtan. Things had changed, she no longer feared him, but that did not change the fact that the terror she first felt had been real. "I was afraid. I thought you would kill me if you knew. I saw you at Frama…"

Brice was shattered that this woman he had just professed to love could believe he would kill her. "If you saw me at Frama, you should know that I killed armed men in battle. I did not murder unarmed women."

"I didn't understand why you attacked my people when we've taken care of you, provided homes and work."

Brice's anger flared. "Provided for us? We provided for you! We fed you, clothed you, built your homes and maintained them. Ryshtans are so ignorant and lazy you can't even blow your own noses without our help. The only thing you are capable of is doling out punishment." Brice's head was spinning. How had a Ryshtan been able to live among them unnoticed? The fact that she had been so ill was the only explanation.

Roslin could see the change come over Brice. His eyes no longer shone with kindness; they flashed hatred. This was the Brice she remembered from Frama, and she lashed out at him. "You murdered my grandfather, Governor Gage."

Brice shook his head. "I'm sorry to say that I was deprived of the pleasure of fighting that murdering coward." It dawned on Brice that she had called Gage her grandfather. He was well aware that Lord Athol's daughter was named Roslin, but it had never occurred to him until now that this was that same Roslin. Anger and hurt flooded through him. Had he really fallen in love with the daughter of that monster who had killed Elsbeth?

"He was not a coward!" Roslin shouted defensively.

"He was a coward, all right, and a monster. What would you call a man who takes pleasure from the misfortune of others? He tortured and murdered my people long enough; we'll die before returning to a life of servitude to the likes of him."

Roslin couldn't believe what she was hearing. How could Brice expect her to believe his lies? She had never witnessed any tortures, and execution was only dealt to those who committed heinous crimes. "He never ordered the murder of innocents. Only criminals are executed as a deterrent to prevent others from following in their path."

"And what crime did my infant sisters commit? Wait...I remember...the crime of having a rapist for a father."

"That's a lie...my grandfather would not order the murder of an innocent baby."

"Your grandfather took my mother as his bed slave. She bore him two daughters who were taken from her and murdered.

Brice found it hard to believe that a highborn Ryshtan would be that naïve. Could it be that they hid such things from their women? "Your grandfather was not alone. Ryshtan men take our women to their beds against their will as bed slaves. When a child results, it's killed. My own Cadie would have been murdered if Lord Athol had known that Elsbeth carried his child."

"I don't believe you. You're trying to turn me against my own people." Roslin remembered how like her younger brother Cadie had seemed when they first met. Could it be true? Was Cadie her sister?

"This discussion is over. I've decided to let your punishment fit the crime. Your people have enslaved mine for generations. You seem to believe that by enslaving my people, the Ryshtans were doing us a favor. I'll extend to you the same favor. You pretended to be a slave, now you'll experience what it's like to be one." Brice took Roslin by the arm and dragged her back to camp and over to the cook fire. He picked up one of the iron rods used to place and remove pots from over the fire, plunging it into the coals to heat.

Roslin's eyes grew wide with fright. "What are you going to do?"

Brice pulled up his shirtsleeve to expose a prominent scar on his upper arm. "I'm sure you've seen many of these before, all my people carry them." He tightened his grip as Roslin's panic grew, and she struggled to get away. "Delano, Lester," Brice called, "come hold her still."

Roslin watched Brice pull the iron out of the hot coals. It was glowing red, and her heart seemed to stop at the thought of it searing into her skin. Never in her life had she known this kind of fear, and she could feel the bile burn her throat. She forced herself to stop struggling. She would not give Brice the satisfaction of seeing her fight and call for mercy.

Closing her eyes, she held her breath and waited. When the hot iron seared her flesh, her legs almost buckled and her scream could be heard throughout the camp. She could smell the burning, and it nauseated her. When it was finished, they released her and she collapsed to the ground, the tears flowing freely down her face as she tried to choke back her sobs.

Brice tossed the iron rod aside and strode back to his tent, retrieving a shirt and ripping it. He took it to his new slave and threw it at her. "This shirt needs mending. Have it finished before the evening meal."

"I don't know how to sew," Roslin managed through her tears.

"I would advise you to learn quickly then. A non-productive slave will not be tolerated." Brice reached down and grabbed her, pulling her to her feet. Addressing the crowd that had gathered, he announced, "This woman has masqueraded as one of us, but she is Ryshtan. She is now my slave and will be treated as such." He released his hold on Roslin, then nodded at the shirt. "Get to work."

Roslin didn't know what to do. She didn't want to make Brice angry, and she clutched the shirt to her as she made her way to Brice's tent, hoping to find Shea there. The woman had been kind to her, and she hoped she would continue to be.

The older woman looked up as Roslin entered the tent. She had heard the commotion outside and knew what had happened. She held a jar of salve out to the young woman. "This will help with the pain." She then picked up a needle and thread and handed them to her, as well. Brice had instructed that she be treated as a slave. In Ryshta, slaves were not spoken to except to be given a task or to be punished. There could be no more conversations with the young woman. She walked out, leaving Roslin alone in her pain.

Roslin's arm was throbbing, and it was hard to think of anything else but the pain. Her stomach told her it was time for the evening meal, and she looked at the shirt in her lap. She had already pulled the thread out and started over three times, yet it still looked awful. She heard the booted footsteps as Brice entered the tent, and she cringed. Brice snatched the shirt and held it up to inspect it.

"Pathetic," he said. He pulled her to her feet and ripped her shirt from her body. "You will wear your handiwork so all will see your ineptitude." He watched as Roslin pulled the shirt over her head. She looked like a child playing dress-up in the large garment. Brice pushed her toward the door. "It's time for the evening meal."

Roslin walked to the cook fire and filled a plate. When she brought a bite to her mouth, the spoon was slapped out of her hand.

"What do you think you're doing?" Brice asked the startled woman.

"I was eating."

"Have you ever seen a slave eat?"

Roslin looked around the campsite filled with people eating their meals. "Yes," she said, indicating with her head the people around her.

"These are not slaves," Brice spat at her. "We are free people." He repeated his question. "Have you ever seen a slave eat?"

Roslin realized that Brice was right; she had never seen one of the palace slaves eat. She never thought about it before. It never seemed important to wonder if they ate or not, as long as they were there to serve her. She felt ashamed that she had never considered their feelings at all.

"No."

"What did your slaves do at meal time?"

Roslin cringed. "They served me my meal."

Brice glared at her. "And what are you now?"

"A slave."

Brice grabbed her shirt and pulled her almost off her feet. "A slave, what? How do you address me?"

"I'm a slave, Master Brice," Roslin corrected, trying to keep her voice steady.

"And what are you here to do?"

"I'm here to serve you, Master Brice."

Brice nodded and released his grip on Roslin's shirt. "When it's meal time, you will serve me. When the meal is finished, you will clean up. When your work is finished, you eat. I expect you to anticipate my every desire without being told. Do you understand?"

"Yes, Master Brice." Roslin was not sure what Brice meant by the word *desire*, but she was afraid to ask him and risk his wrath again. All she could assume was that she was to serve him as a bed slave, as well.

She walked over and got another plate that she filled for Brice. When she handed it to him, he nodded to Shea and a puzzled Cadie, who had joined him at the fire. The little girl had been at the other side of camp playing with her cousins and could not understand her papa's harsh treatment of her friend. Immediately, Roslin filled two more plates and served the rest of the master's family.

"Why is Papa so mad?" Cadie asked Roslin when she handed her a plate.

"You're not to talk to Roslin anymore, Cadie," Brice said, pulling the child away.

"But why, Papa? Roslin is my friend."

"Not anymore," Brice answered, as he abruptly stood and quickly walked away, unable to face his heartbroken daughter.

When the meal was finished, Shea ushered a reluctant Cadie to their tent. Roslin was left to clean up and wonder what a bed slave actually does. When she was finally finished, she retired into the shadows with a hunk of bread and some gravy, not wanting to risk being seen eating.

When she got back to the tent, Shea and Cadie had retired for the night. Cadie slipped out of bed and quietly approached Roslin, who was sitting forlornly on her cot. "Why don't you want to be my friend?" the child asked, a tear starting down her cheek. "Don't you like me anymore?"

Roslin pulled the sad little girl into her arms. "No matter what happens, you'll always be my friend, don't ever forget that." She stroked the child's head and rocked her back and forth. "I didn't tell your papa something important. Now he's mad at me, but it has nothing to do with you. I don't want you to get in trouble because of me, so please don't talk to me when he's around. Now get back to bed before he finds us together." She kissed Cadie on the forehead and sent her on her way.

Roslin knew it would not be long before Brice would retire. *Should I wait on my cot for him till he calls for me? No...he said anticipate his desires without being asked. I have to be waiting for him when he gets back.* Reluctantly, she disrobed and walked around the screen to his cot and slipped under the blanket. Roslin had been attracted to the man and had believed she was falling in love with him. She had wondered and fantasized about what it would be like to make love with him, but this was different. She was repulsed by the thought of her body being used for the pleasure of someone who had grown to despise her.

Brice started back to his tent and wondered why he felt the need to be so hard on Roslin. He didn't seem to be able to help it. He just couldn't separate his feelings for Lord Athol from his daughter. The thought that he had been attracted to that monster's child was hard to accept. He entered the tent and stepped behind the screen and sat on the cot to remove his boots. He felt Roslin immediately and jumped up and turned to face her.

Cold fury pumped through his body. He grabbed the edge of the cot and tipped it over, dumping Roslin onto the floor. "Your father murdered Cadie's mother, and you think you can take her place in my bed?" He picked up a blanket and threw it on Roslin to cover her nakedness. "He snuffed out her life as if it meant nothing. You disgust me. You Ryshtans have no concept of love or compassion, do you? What does it matter if you destroy a few lives, so long as your needs are met?"

"No…I'm sorry," Roslin stammered. "You said I was to serve your every desire. I thought that meant in your bed, as well." She stood and wrapped the blanket around her body. "I know you don't believe me, but I'm so sorry for what my people did to you. I understand now what it's like to be a slave."

"You understand nothing! A lifetime of suffering cannot be comprehended in the few hours you've been a slave."

Roslin realized that Brice was right. She could not possibly understand what a lifetime of this type of treatment would do to a people. But she had been a slave long enough to feel the helplessness and humiliation it caused. Her eyes filled with tears, and she put her face in her hands and sobbed. To realize she had treated people as her possessions without even giving it a second thought broke her heart. She turned and ran out of the tent.

Brice watched Roslin run away and shuddered at the thought that she believed he wanted to use her as a bed slave. He had been hard on her, yes, but he would never force himself on the woman. He did not have to be raped himself to understand the pain and humiliation it caused. The pain of what Elsbeth had endured flooded back into his consciousness, and he tried to lock it away again in a dark corner of his mind. "I'm so sorry, Elsbeth...I wish I had been able to protect you," he whispered, as the memories refused to be locked away this time.

"I've had enough of this, Brice," Shea said, pulling his thoughts out of the past. "You owe that child an apology."

Brice's mouth fell open. How could she expect him to apologize to a Ryshtan?

"I can't. Mother, you don't understand. She thought I wanted to use her as a bed slave." He closed his eyes and shuddered. "A bed slave." Angry blue eyes tracked to calm brown. "When I think of all that Elsbeth had to endure at the hands of Roslin's father, I want to vomit. What all of our women have endured at the hands of Ryshtans." Brice stood and turned his back to Shea. "She told me she understands what it means to be a slave. She knows nothing!" He turned back, his hands balled into fists. "I won't apologize. It's time one of them learns to walk in our shoes. How appropriate that it's the daughter of the worst of them all."

Shea shook her head. "You're wrong."

Brice sat heavily on the cot, leaned over, and placed his face in his hands. "I knew you wouldn't understand."

"I think I do," Shea said, reaching over to lift his head so she could see his face. "You were attracted to her. You thought you were falling in love, and that made you feel guilty because you thought you were being unfaithful to Elsbeth. While you were trying to work out that guilt, you found out Roslin was Ryshtan and that you were falling for Elsbeth's murderer...the ultimate betrayal. Don't you see? You've been taking out the sins of Roslin's father on her, and that's just not fair." She sat next to Brice and squeezed his hand.

"You have hurt and humiliated her. Any more and you will be no better than the ones we are fighting against. You just made a speech to her about the Ryshtans not caring how their actions hurt our people and how much that disgusted you." Shea took his face in her hands. "Look at yourself, Brice. Do you think because they did it to us first that it makes enslaving them acceptable? I see you becoming more and more like them in your treatment of Roslin, and I can't condone that kind of behavior from a child of mine. I brought you up better than that. Roslin was brought up to think slavery is acceptable. Living here with us was helping her see the error in that. I believe she has a good heart, and her apology to you was sincere."

Brice dropped his gaze to the floor. He had been behaving like the ones he despised most in the world, and the thought sickened him. *God! What am I becoming?* The final insult to Elsbeth's memory would be for him to become no better than the animals who murdered her.

"I'm sorry, Mother…I didn't realize." Brice pulled her in for an embrace. "I can't forget that she's Ryshtan…I just can't. I don't like myself for the way I've treated her, but…" Brice closed his eyes, and a tear trickled down his cheek. "I'll tell her tomorrow that she's no longer a slave, but I don't think I can apologize…not yet." He was still not prepared to fully trust the woman—that would take time—but he could treat her civilly.

Shea squeezed Brice's hand and left him to think things over. She had faith that Brice's heart would eventually win this battle.

Brice sat on his cot, Shea's words playing over and over in his mind. Why did things have to turn out like this? Why had he let himself fall under that woman's spell so quickly? A small voice broke his silent musings.

"Why did you make my friend cry, Papa?" Cadie looked up at Brice sadly.

Brice felt guilt settle heavily on his shoulders. Not only had he behaved badly, he had done it within earshot of his precious Cadie. What kind of an example was he setting for his child? "We had a misunderstanding, but I'm sure it'll work itself out."

"When someone hurts my feelings and I cry, you always talk to me and make me feel better. Please go talk to Roslin, Papa. She needs to feel better."

Brice pulled Cadie into his arms and hugged her tightly. "I will, little one." His daughter had a way of making everything seem so simple. "You go back to bed and I'll go talk to her." He walked Cadie to her cot and tucked her in. Then he left in search of Roslin.

He found her huddled on the ground by the cook tent. She appeared to be asleep, and Brice decided this talk could wait until morning. He would tell her then that she was no longer a slave and that they would set her free to go—or stay—as she chose after the battle for Darius was won.

Roslin saw Brice walking toward her and quickly closed her eyes. Hopefully, whatever task he had for her would be forgotten until morning if he thought the slave was asleep. Roslin listened as the footsteps stopped for a moment, then turned back the way they came.

She had come to realize that she did not begrudge these people their freedom. She understood now that slavery was wrong. She believed that with all her heart and wondered why she had not seen it before. Perhaps it was because her life had been so removed from the plight of the slaves. Roslin was sure if she had really understood what was going on, it would have made a difference. She chastised herself for not caring enough to even try to find out how these people were treated. One thing was for sure, Roslin did not want to continue to be a slave, and she couldn't sit by and let them slaughter her friends and family, either.

A decision was made. She would wait until she was certain everyone slept deeply, then she would slip away and go home and warn her people. Brice had told her how close they were to Darius, and she believed if she left that night, she would be there by late afternoon or early evening the next day.

When the camp had been quiet for some time, Roslin got up and slipped into the cook tent. She grabbed a loaf of bread and a jug of water, then walked silently to Brice's tent. She had run out of there with just the blanket wrapped around her naked body and needed to retrieve her clothes and sandals before she could begin her journey. She prayed that Brice was not a light sleeper and that she could get in and out without disturbing him. Afraid to even breathe, she crept to where she had left her clothes and scooped them up. She didn't take a breath again until she was safely outside. Slipping into the shadows at the edge of camp, Roslin dropped the blanket and dressed quickly. She didn't know how soon they would discover her missing, but she hoped she would have at least a few hours head start.

The sun was just coming up when Roslin heard a noise behind her and ducked into the underbrush to hide. It sounded like someone had stepped on a twig and broken it. Her mouth went dry and her heart pounded. What if it was Brice coming to drag her back to camp? She held her breath and tried to be as quiet as possible.

Just then, she saw Cadie running along, her eyes frantically scanning the path ahead. She stood and grabbed the girl as she ran by. "What are you doing here?" Roslin asked, angry at herself for not noticing that she was being followed.

Cadie wrapped her arms around Roslin and squeezed her tightly. "Don't be mad that I followed you. I love you. I don't want you to go. Please don't leave us."

Roslin didn't know what to do. They had been walking for hours, and there was no way she could take the child back. As mad as Brice would be at her for running away, he would kill her for taking his daughter.

She thought about the life Cadie had led until now, not having a home, traveling from battle to battle. That was no life for a child. But was taking her away from the only family she had ever known right? Roslin thought of the times she had seen Brice with Cadie. The love that shone in his eyes was real, and the child was not even his true daughter. Roslin had never seen her father's eyes light up like that at the sight of her.

No, as much as I would like to have my sister with me, I can't take her away from Brice. It would break his heart. A decision was made; she could not go back, but somehow, she would find a way to get Cadie back to her father.

"I'm sorry, but I can't go back, Cadie. I'm going to see my father." She took the girl's hand and led her away from the road. With the child along, the chances of Brice following her went from probable to certain, and she decided they would walk out of sight of the road.

"I'm hungry," Cadie said, looking up expectantly.

Roslin had planned on eating as she walked, not wanting any delay that could allow Brice to catch up with her. But now things had changed. She needed to let Cadie rest or she wouldn't make it without being carried, and Roslin didn't think she was strong enough to carry the child any distance. They would take a short break to rest and eat. Walking to a tree, she sat down, leaning her back against it. She wasn't aware of how tired she was until she sat, grateful to be off her feet. Breaking the small loaf, she handed Cadie half.

Roslin stuffed the last bite of bread in her mouth and brushed the crumbs off her dress. "We have to get going, Cadie. We still have a long way to walk."

"I'm tired."

"I know you're tired, but we have to go." She knew if Brice wasn't already up that he soon would be. Once he found Cadie gone, he would be on her trail. She had to get the child up and walking again.

Roslin stood and pulled Cadie to her feet.

"I want to go back to my papa."

"I told you I can't go back. You're going to have to come with me." She grabbed Cadie's hand and walked toward the morning sun.

Cadie started to cry. "I want my papa," she sobbed, as Roslin pulled her along.

Roslin stopped and knelt in front of Cadie. "Sweetie, I promise I'll get you back to your papa, but first we have to go and see mine. Okay?"

Cadie continued to cry and Roslin tried to think of something to quiet her down. If she kept this up, Brice could find her with no problem. "You know, I sure would love to hear one of your stories, Cadie. You tell them so well."

The little girl stopped crying and gave a crooked smile. She loved the way Roslin praised her stories and immediately started into a tall tale. They took turns telling stories until Roslin finally started to see familiar landscape. When they reached Darius, she was carrying the child. Exhausted and hungry, Roslin thought her arms would break off.

Instead of turning toward the palace, Roslin walked toward the slave village. She knew that once she told her father about the slave rebellion, none of these people would be safe. As much as she had tried not to believe Brice's words, Roslin had come to the conclusion that he did indeed speak the truth.

Verda Foster

Chapter 5

Brice woke but lay in bed thinking about his actions the night before. Power with nothing to balance it is a dangerous thing. He had succumbed to it without even realizing it. He shuddered at the thought of how much like the Ryshtans he had allowed himself to become. He was grateful to his mother for stepping in and forcing him to see what he was doing.

He stood and stretched his tall frame, then reached for his clothes. This was going to be the last day of the journey that had started five years ago when Elsbeth died. They would reach the outskirts of Darius that night and make camp.

It seemed the closer he got to where it all started, the more on edge Brice became. He hated Lord Athol with every fiber of his being, and the thought that he would finally be able to get his revenge was intoxicating. This quest had taken its toll, dividing Brice's family. His father, mother, and oldest brother had both followed him, and his father had fallen in battle a year into their journey. The three middle brothers had chosen to stay in Darius, not believing that Brice could truly be The Chosen. They feared that to follow Brice would mean death. The reunion would be bittersweet.

Brice stepped around the privacy screen and found all three cots empty. He walked to the tent flap, only to be met by Shea coming in, concern showing in her eyes. "Mother...what's wrong?"

"Have you seen Roslin or Cadie?" Shea asked.

"No, I just got up. Have you looked everywhere?" Shea nodded, and Brice pushed past her to make a search of his own. The camp was quiet, most of the people still in slumber. Walking the perimeter of the camp, he found the blanket Roslin had been wrapped in the last time he had seen her. Her footsteps were headed away from camp, toward Darius. Brice's heart stopped, and real panic set in when he saw the small footprints of his little girl walking in the same direction.

"No!" Brice screamed, as he crumpled to the ground. "She took my baby." Pictures flashed through his mind of what Lord Athol would do to Cadie if he got his hands on her. His grief was soon replaced by blind fury, as he got up and ran to Glen's tent. He pulled his brother out of bed and dragged him outside. "Roslin has run away to warn the sovereign, and she's taken Cadie with her. I'm going after them. I don't know how much of a lead they have on me, but they're on foot. I'm going to try to stop them before they reach Darius. You're in charge here. When you get to Darius, don't make camp and wait. Start the attack immediately."

"What about you?"

"Don't worry about me. I'll find Cadie and get her to safety, then I'll join you." Brice began to saddle his mount. "Get everyone up and going, every moment we delay gives them more time to prepare a defense." With those words, he mounted up and was gone.

Roslin made her way to a largish building and found a group of women inside sitting and sewing. Some were stitching fine silk garments, and some were weaving cloth. An older woman looked up at her with a puzzled expression.

"I don't remember seeing you before. Why are you out and about when the bell has not sounded?"

Roslin placed the sleeping child on the floor and turned to face the woman. "I'm here to help you," she said. "Do any of you know a tall man named Brice?" Gasps were heard all around the room, as all eyes turned to the stranger, who asked of their lost friend.

One woman spoke up. "Yes, we knew Brice. Why do you ask about someone who has been dead for five years?"

"Brice isn't dead. He's on his way here now with an army to try to defeat the sovereign."

The woman shook her head. "Brice tried to get our men to join with him. Some followed him, and they were all slaughtered."

"Did you see their bodies?"

"The sovereign said they didn't deserve a proper burial, and he left their bodies for the vultures."

"He lied. I just left Brice yesterday. He's alive and well."

The woman crossed her arms over her chest. "How do we know you speak the truth?"

Roslin pointed to the child sleeping on the floor. "This is his daughter, Cadie. When she wakes, she can tell you her father is alive."

A woman in the back of the room stood, and all eyes turned to her. She walked to the sleeping girl and knelt down and stroked the auburn hair that was so like Elsbeth's. "Cadie?" Tears started down her face as she watched the girl sleep. "I thought my grandchild was dead."

"You're Elsbeth's mother?"

"Yes." The woman stood and extended her hand. "I'm Cora."

Roslin was pleased that she could leave Cadie in the care of her grandmother, knowing she would be in loving hands. "Cora, I need Cadie to stay with you. I didn't know that she had followed me until it was too late to return her. Please get her safely back to Brice." She looked around the room, her eyes pleading with them to believe her. "I have an important message for you all. Spread the word that Brice is on his way here with an army. You need to get your families out of the city as soon as you can. You're all in danger if you stay. The battle could begin as early as tonight, but no later than first light in the morning. You don't have a lot of time."

"We'll all be killed," a voice from the back of the room said.

"Not if you stay calm," Roslin responded quickly, before panic could spread. "You need to go on with your work like nothing is happening. It won't be long until the bell sounds. As soon as it does, go home and gather your families and get out. Don't take time to gather your belongings, just get out. Hopefully, you will all be long gone before the fighting starts."

Roslin knew that when she warned her father about the rebel army, he would no doubt try to round up the slaves of Darius to use as a shield. She couldn't live with herself if they were all butchered because of her actions. No, she was glad she had warned them so they could get to safety. Now the problem was time. She didn't know how much she had but was certain it was not much. She would wait to warn her father until at least an hour after the bell sounded. She hoped that would give the slaves enough time to get away yet give her people a chance to prepare for battle.

Brice was riding hard when his horse stumbled and almost went down. He checked over the lathered animal and found that the horse was favoring his right front hoof. He picked it up and removed a stone that was wedged into the frog. "Damn!" he shouted, and kicked a nearby sapling, breaking it off near the ground. The horse jumped at the sudden disturbance, and Brice patted his neck to calm him down. "I'm sorry, Angus," he said as he slipped the bridle off the horse's head. He removed the saddle, as well, and rubbed the big animal's jaw. "I'll be back for you as soon as I can."

Brice knew better than to treat a horse like this, but Cadie's life was at stake. He broke into an easy jog, realizing that he needed to pace himself or end up just like Angus. It would do Cadie no good if he collapsed and didn't make it at all. The fact that he hadn't caught them yet confirmed his fears that they had left the previous night and not early that morning as he had hoped. Undoubtedly, they would already be in the city by now, but they would not be expecting Brice's army to arrive until late that night. He could still slip in and get Cadie out if Athol hadn't already murdered her. *Pacing be damned*, he thought, and picked up speed.

Roslin approached the palace with much trepidation. The guilt she felt knowing that she was about to betray Brice and the people she had grown to care for was overwhelming. She couldn't think of any other way. She couldn't stand to see a repeat of what happened at Frama. She saw a group of slaves bringing fresh produce into the palace and joined them, fearing the guards would not let her enter. Once inside, she quickly walked to her father's chamber and knocked on the door. *Well, it's too late to change my mind now.*

"My God, girl, what happened to you?" Athol shouted. "Why are you dressed in those rags?" He saw a red discoloration on her upper arm and pulled her close to examine the blemish. "Who dared to brand my daughter like a common slave?" Rage flashed in his eyes. The humiliation of his seed walking around branded was overwhelming.

"The slaves have mobilized into a rebellion, Father. Grandfather Gage is dead, and Frama has fallen. I was trying to get home to you, and the rebels found me. They thought I was one of them, but when they discovered I was Ryshtan, I was forced to be the slave of their leader Brice. I managed to escape and came home to warn you."

"He used you as his slave?" Athol shook his head in disgust. He would never be able to marry her off now. No man would have a woman who was used in this manner. "Cover that up, girl; I don't want it public knowledge that those barbarians used you as a slave. I would never live down the shame."

"Yes, Father," Roslin answered, trying to stretch her sleeve to cover the burn.

"Brice...that name is familiar. Wasn't he a trainer in my stables?" Athol glanced at Lennix, his slave boss, for confirmation and received a nod.

"Brice is the slave who went berserk over the death of your runaway bed slave," Lennix answered. "The girl and her father were executed and hung out as an example of what happens to runaways and anyone who harbors them."

"Ah, yes, now I remember. Brice was a bad one, all right. He ran away, too, taking a good many of my able-bodied slaves with him." He turned back to Roslin. "We let it be known that they had been hunted down and killed to prevent others from trying to follow and join them."

"May I be excused to clean myself up and put on some appropriate clothes?"

"By all means, get out of those rags," Athol said, "and try not to let anyone else see you until you look decent."

"Yes, Father," she said, and hurried from the room. She had given her people a fighting chance. That's what she had come here to do, so why did she feel guilty about it? She wished she could think of a way to stop the battle without bloodshed. She didn't want the Ryshtans to win, but she didn't want them slaughtered, either.

Roslin walked to her room in silence. The regret she felt at warning her father seemed to hover around her shoulders, weighing them down. If Brice didn't hate her before, he certainly would now. Now that she understood the pain he had been through, she understood why he had lashed out at her. If only there was something she could do to stop the fighting. A thought came to her; if she could just put her father's soldiers out of commission…Yes, that could work. She hurried to her room to change, so she could set her plan in motion.

Roslin knocked on the door and waited for the healer to answer. This had to work, so much depended on it. The door opened, and the raven-haired Belvin greeted her. He was a rather obese man, with thick bushy eyebrows. His cheeks and nose were always flushed, giving the appearance of long hours in the sun. He looked at her with surprise. The young woman was supposed to be in Frama.

"What can I do for you, my lady?" he asked, bowing his head to show respect. She looked haggard, and there were dark circles under her eyes.

"I'm in need of a strong sleeping powder, Belvin. I think I shall go mad if I don't get some rest."

"Of course, my lady. Come in, I have just the thing." He stepped aside to welcome her inside. He turned and led the way to a room that was full of bottles and jugs of every size and shape. He walked to a large jug and scooped out a spoonful of powder and emptied it on a square of paper, which he folded up and slipped into a cloth pouch. "Put a pinch of this in some water or juice and drink it down. It should do the trick, but be sure not to put it into wine. When mixed with spirits, it's ten times more potent, and it'll knock you right out, with a most unpleasant headache when you finally awaken."

Just what I need, she thought. "I'll be careful," Roslin answered, reaching out to take the pouch. "Thank you." Now she just needed to figure out how she would get back in here to get that jug of sleeping powder without being seen. That problem was solved when someone pounded on the door and asked the healer to rush to his wife's bedside. She was about to give birth to their first child, and the man was all in a dither. The two men rushed away, leaving Roslin to collect the powder unhampered.

The final part of Roslin's plan would kill two birds with one stone. The slaves who lived within the palace grounds had not been warned and sent to safety. She would need their help to drug the wine and get it to the soldiers. There was no way she could get it all done in time by herself. Slipping out of the palace, she went to the slave cottages in the back. If she could not get these people to believe her, all would be lost.

She knocked at the door of the first cottage, silently praying that her plan could be carried out in time. The door opened, and a fair-haired child stared at Roslin. "Who is it, Elise?" a voice asked, as the child's mother appeared at the door.

"I need your help, Lena," Roslin said, recognizing the woman as one of her own personal servants.

The woman knelt and asked, "How may I serve you, my lady?"

Lena's husband arrived at the door and dropped to his knee, as well.

"I came to warn you that you're in grave danger and to ask for your help in preventing bloodshed between your people and mine."

The couple did not rise, afraid to be caught standing in the presence of the sovereign's family. The man looked at her skeptically. "Why would you want to help us?"

Roslin lifted her sleeve and showed them the brand on her arm. "I don't have time to explain everything right now, but please trust me when I tell you I'm here to help. Slavery is wrong, and I want to do what I can to stop it." Roslin could see by the shocked expression on the man's face that the sight of her burned arm had had the desired effect.

"A runaway slave called Brice is on his way here with an army to destroy Darius. If this happens, there will be many casualties on both sides."

The slave's expression had changed from skepticism to wanting to believe, then back to skepticism at the mention of Brice's name. "Brice can't lead an army; he died five years ago."

"He's alive. I spent the last few weeks with him and his family," Roslin said, hoping desperately that they would believe her and help. Time was running out.

Lena grasped her husband's arm. "It can't be."

"I don't have time to argue with you about Brice's death," Roslin continued. "There's an army approaching, and lives will be lost unless we do something. I have a plan that can prevent this, but I need your help to drug my father's best wine and deliver it to the soldiers so they'll be unable to join in the fight. Round up all the palace slaves and send the women and children away. The rest of you can help me stop the soldiers."

The young husband found it hard to believe that the sovereign's daughter would help them like this, but she seemed sincere, and he found himself trusting her. He stood and extended his hand. "My name is Rogan, and I'm proud to help you, Lady Roslin."

"Thank you," Roslin said, taking his hand and squeezing. "Please hurry, we don't have much time."

Roslin sat at Rogan's side as he drove the wagon full of wine toward the palace gates. *This has to work*, she thought, glancing at the crates behind her. They stopped at the gate, and the palace guard greeted Lady Roslin with a bow. Roslin acknowledged the bow and said, "Open the gates. My father is sending his finest wine so his noble soldiers can drink a toast to victory before the battle. Of course the royal guards, such as yourself, will have the honor of drinking their toast with the sovereign himself and not have to settle for his daughter."

She was relieved to see the grin spread on his face as he opened the gates and waved them through. They drove the wagon to the soldier's enclosure, and Rogan helped Roslin down. Men were bustling around busily, preparing for battle, but stopped in their tracks when they saw Lady Roslin. Taking a deep breath, Roslin began to speak.

"Good soldiers of Ryshta, my father wishes to honor you by presenting you with his finest wine. He has every confidence in your victory over the ragtag rebels who threaten our sovereignty. He has asked that every one of you drink a toast to the coming victory." Roslin extended her hand to the wagon.

The soldiers quickly lined up to unload the wagon, and Roslin beckoned Rogan to follow her, leaving the men to distribute the wine and carry out what they believed to be the sovereign's wishes. When they were out of sight of the soldiers, Roslin stopped and turned to Rogan. "It's time for you to join your family in safety. Thank you." Rogan started to kneel in front of her, and Roslin took his hand and pulled him back up. "You're a free man now. You no longer need to kneel before the likes of me."

Rogan dropped to his knee. "I'm honored to have been of service to you, Lady Roslin." He took her hand and kissed it. "I say this as a free man, and I kneel because I want to, not because I have to."

A tear came to Roslin's eye. "Thank you. Now get to safety, your family will be worried."

"What about you, my lady?"

"I have to go back and try to keep my father occupied until I know the drug has had time to work. I'm hoping when he finds out, he'll see he has no choice but to surrender. If we're lucky, this could be over soon with no one getting hurt."

"Luck be with you then, my lady," Rogan said, as he stood to leave.

Roslin watched him until he was out of sight, then started back to the palace. It looked like things just might work out. She hoped that once Cadie got back to Brice, and Rogan explained everything else, perhaps he could forgive her for unintentionally spiriting away his daughter. Roslin knew he had to be frantic with worry over the child, and she was sorry for causing him such grief.

Brice was almost to the palace and his goal. He knew he should feel exhausted, but the adrenaline pumping through him made him oblivious to the fatigue. It seemed the closer he got, the more energy he felt. All he could think of was finding Cadie. Once he knew his little girl was safe, Roslin and her father would pay.

He reached the palace and slipped over the wall unnoticed. *Pathetic*, he thought. The Ryshtans had grown so complacent, even a child would have no trouble sneaking in. Brice had never been a palace slave and was not familiar with the grounds. Having no idea where to start, he decided to go from room to room until he found Cadie. Anyone who tried to stop him would pay dearly. He had just started through the garden when he caught movement out of the corner of his eye. Glancing over, he saw that Roslin was also walking toward the palace.

At the same moment, Roslin saw Brice and froze. She recognized the look in Brice's eyes for what it was. It was clear that Brice meant to kill her, and she turned to run. He easily overtook her and threw her to the ground. He straddled Roslin and placed his dagger against her throat.

"Tell me where Cadie is," Brice demanded, as he pushed the blade until blood trickled down Roslin's neck.

"I went to the slaves and gave her to her grandmother. I told them you were coming and asked that they take Cadie back to you."

Brice found it hard to believe this incredible story. Why would Roslin take Cadie only to send her back? It made no sense. No, she had taken the child to use against them when the battle started, and Brice would not let that happen. Roslin would tell where Cadie was, then she would die. "Don't lie to me! I'll kill you and anyone else who keeps me from my daughter."

"I told you the truth. I would never hurt Cadie. I love her."

Brice was trembling, he was so angry. He had believed that Roslin was falling in love with him before all this started, and that turned out to be a lie. She was only pretending until she could run away and warn her father of their plans. Now to hear the woman profess to love Cadie was too much. "I hope you've made peace with your God because you're about to die." Brice lifted the dagger into the air and made ready to plunge it into his betrayer's heart.

Roslin watched Brice's trembling hands as she waited for the dagger to strike. They seemed to hover above her forever, prolonging the agony. "Just do it and get it over with!" she screamed, as she reached up and grabbed Brice's hands, forcing them down toward her chest.

Startled, Brice watched as the tip of the knife broke through the skin of Roslin's chest. "No!" he shouted, as he pulled the dagger back, then tossed it to the side. Roslin watched Brice's expression change from one of fury to one of pain. "Why did you steal my baby?" he asked, a tear starting down his face. "I loved you."

Roslin pulled up the sleeve on her right arm to expose raw burned skin. "You have a funny way of showing it."

He got off Roslin and sat, his eyes never leaving her face. "I'm sorry I did that, but...I was hurt and angry." Brice looked down at his hands as the tears continued to fall. "I thought we were growing to love each other. I cared about you, and you lied to me." Looking back into Roslin's eyes, he pleaded. "Please, I don't want to hurt you, I just want my baby. Give her to me and you'll never have to see me again."

Roslin couldn't believe how vulnerable Brice had allowed himself to become. She couldn't bear to see the pain reflected in his eyes. She reached over and covered one of his large hands with her own. "Please believe me. I didn't steal Cadie from you. I would never do that. When I ran away, she followed me. I didn't know until it was too late. I couldn't go back, and I couldn't leave her alone, so I brought her with me. I told you the truth. I gave her to your people and asked them to warn the others, then get Cadie back to the safety of your camp." She squeezed Brice's hand. "Cadie is safe."

Brice searched the green depths of Roslin's eyes. He wanted so desperately to believe what she said. A lifetime of hate and mistrust of the Ryshtans made it difficult to believe that one of them would protect his child, especially after the way Brice had treated Roslin when he found out the truth about her. He felt relief wash over him as he realized that he did trust Roslin. Cadie was safe. Brice took a deep breath and closed his eyes, wiping the tears from his face. "Thank you," he whispered.

"You've got to leave," Roslin said. "It's not safe for you here."

Brice nodded and stood to go.

"Wait," Roslin said, standing quickly and grabbing Brice's arm. She was torn as to whether or not to tell Brice what she had done. If her feelings were correct about the rebel leader, Brice would help her take down Ryshta with as little bloodshed as possible. But what if she was wrong? It would be the slaughter she had been trying to prevent. "I…"

"Yes?"

"I sent drugged wine to my father's soldiers to drink a toast to victory. They should still be unconscious when your army arrives."

Brice looked into sincere green eyes. "Why?"

"I was trying to prevent bloodshed…on your side and mine."

"Do you know what you've done? Your father will never forgive you for this."

"I don't seek my father's forgiveness…only yours."

Brice shook his head. "I'm the one who needs to ask forgiveness. Can you forgive me for the way I treated you when I found out you were Ryshtan?"

A tear started down Roslin's cheek. "I can," she answered, never breaking eye contact.

Brice wiped the tear away with his thumb. "And I can forgive you," he said. "I need to get back to my army and let them know the situation before all hell breaks loose around here."

Brice pulled Roslin into his arms and pressed his lips to her forehead in a gentle kiss. He closed his eyes and clung to the young woman, not wanting to let go. "In the barn, there's a grain storage room. Three paces from the south wall, there's a door in the floor that can be pulled up. Look for a nick in one of the floorboards. That's how you pry it open. It leads to an underground room that I built to hide Elsbeth until I could find a safe place for her and the baby. Promise me you'll go to the safety of the room until this is over. I'm afraid of what your father will do to you if he finds out what you've done."

"I promise."

Brice leaned down for one more kiss, then he was gone.

The captain of the royal guard knelt before his sovereign. Alban was visibly shaken by the news he was to relay to Lord Athol. His lord was known for his temper and frequently took it out on the messenger of bad news. "My lord, we searched the village, and the slaves are nowhere to be found."

"What?" Athol bellowed. Anger flushed his face. Somehow the slaves had been warned and had managed to escape.

"There is more to report, my lord. It would appear that someone drugged the wine you sent to your army for a victory toast. We found the men unconscious at their posts."

"I sent no wine!" Athol pounded his fist on the table, furious at the turn of events.

"But the guard at the palace gate told me that Lady Roslin personally told him it was from you."

"Roslin?" How could this be? There must be some misunderstanding. "Find her…bring her to me."

"Yes, my lord."

Athol was stunned. Would his own daughter try to undermine their defenses? It couldn't be. She was, after all, Ryshtan. There had to be something else at work here, and he intended to find out what—or who—it was. He needed to think, clear his head. Walking outside into the cool moonlit night, he sought the solitude of his garden. Hearing voices, he slipped behind the hedge that bordered the garden. He could see Roslin standing with the rebel leader Brice. When the slave kissed her and she did not try to rebuff him, it was more than Athol could stand. She was the daughter of the sovereign; he was a piece of low-life trash.

Suddenly, he understood why all the slaves had vanished. Roslin had betrayed him. How could she choose to side with them? The bastards had even branded her, yet she was helping them. If he'd had some of the royal guard with him, he would have had Brice captured on the spot, but looking at the size of the man, there was no way he would try to take him on alone. No, he would wait until he left, then deal with Roslin.

Roslin watched Brice disappear into the darkness. The world she grew up in was crumbling around her, yet she smiled. All she could think of was that Brice did not hate her, had actually asked for her forgiveness. Not only did she forgive him, she was grateful to him for opening her eyes to the suffering the Ryshtans had caused.

"Well, well. What do we have here? My daughter, willingly consorting with the enemy."

Roslin whirled around to face her father. She watched as he slowly approached her, a look of pure hatred reflected in his eyes. "Father, I—"

"Shut up!" Athol shouted, as he slapped her across the face. "I don't need to hear any excuses from your betraying lips. Anything you say would be a lie. You let that low-class scum touch you. I saw the look on your face when that bastard kissed you. You enjoyed it." He backhanded her hard, his ring leaving a bloody scrape across her face. He reached down and grabbed her arm and started for the palace, pulling her with him. "He may take Darius from me, but he won't take you. When he returns, he'll find his new woman hanging out on display, just like the other one."

Roslin couldn't believe this was happening. Her father meant to kill her and hang her out to torment Brice. Frantically, she pulled away and tried to run, but he grabbed her again, and this time, she felt his fist slam into her face before everything went black.

Verda Foster

Chapter 6

Brice went over the wall again and started away from the palace at an easy jog. He headed for the woods east of the city, sure that he would find the recent evacuees in its protective cover. Glen and the rest of the army would not arrive for some time yet, but he could start to organize the men of Darius who were willing to fight.

He was not sure how many would join him; after all, these were the ones who had been afraid to follow him five years ago when he ran away and started building and training an army that would one day bring an end to the reign of the sovereign.

He reached the woods and moved silently, listening for any sound that would lead him to the hidden slaves. He was almost to the other side of the woods when he heard voices and crept closer to verify that these were his people. Brice smiled as he recognized friends he'd not seen in five years. His long strides carried him swiftly toward the large group of people who sat and waited for word that Brice's army had arrived. In the center of the group stood an older man who gestured animatedly as he spoke.

Brice couldn't see the man's face, but he recognized the voice. It was Mikah, the head elder and his main opponent when he was attempting to convince the slaves of Darius to join together to defeat the Ryshtans. Brice could tell by his tone that he was not pleased with the turn of events. The old man saw him approaching and walked to meet him.

Brice had never been able to get through to the village elder, and by the sound of it, he was still advising the people of Darius that to follow Brice would mean death. It was also evident that they were no longer willing to listen to him now that it appeared Brice had in fact been The Chosen all along.

"Well," the old man said, "I see the rumors are true." He looked around to see if anyone accompanied Brice. "Where is this army of yours that's come to liberate us?"

"I came ahead. They'll be here tonight," Brice answered, looking through the throng of people. More and more were gathering, as word spread that he had arrived. He heard someone shouting his name, and Brice turned to see his brother Collin running toward him.

Collin threw his arms around Brice in welcome. "They told us you had all been hunted down and killed," he said. He stepped back and took a good look at Brice. "You are a sight for sore eyes." He hugged him again. "Come on, I'll take you to see the rest of the family." He smiled and turned to lead the way.

"Is Cadie with you?" Brice asked as he fell in step with his brother.

"Yes, Cora brought her when she gave us the news that you were coming. Cadie is going to be so glad to see you. I think she was a little bewildered to wake up among so many strangers."

They continued through the crowd of people who had come to see for themselves that Brice was really there. Everyone wanted to hug him or shake his hand and thank him for coming back for them. It was slow going, but finally, the people he found surrounding him were family. He could see his brother Dover standing away in the shadows watching, but he made no move to greet Brice. Brice felt a pang of regret at the way they had parted and knew when this was all over he would probably have to make the first move to re-establish a relationship with his brother.

"Papa," Cadie shouted, running as fast as her little legs could carry her.

Brice knelt down and scooped the child up in his arms. They had been apart for only one day, but it had been agony. "You scared me when you ran off like that," he said, as he hugged Cadie fiercely. "Please don't ever leave again without telling me where you're going. It's important I know where you are or I worry."

"I was okay, Papa, I was with Roslin," Cadie said, wondering why her father would be worried about her when she was with her friend.

Brice felt arms wrapping around him as his brother Rylan greeted him.

"It's about time you got back," Rylan said, punching his arm. "When this is all over, we have a lot of catching up to do. You have a niece and nephew you've never met." He brushed a lock of wild red hair out of his eyes and looked around. "Are Mother and Father with you? And where's Glen?"

"Mother and Glen are on their way here now, but..." Brice looked down sadly. "Father was killed four years ago."

The brothers became quiet as the sad news was digested. They had accepted their family's death five years before, but hope that the whole family would be reunited had blossomed with the news that Brice and his army were on their way home.

"I know you all want to know what happened to Father and I'll tell you everything, but this isn't the time. We have to get organized and prepare for what's to come." Collin and Rylan nodded in agreement, and Brice continued. "I believe we'll be able to take Darius with little or no bloodshed." He saw the skeptical look on their faces and hastened to explain. "Lady Roslin managed to drug most of the sovereign's army. All that remain are the royal guard, and when my army arrives, we'll have them vastly outnumbered."

"Are you sure we can trust her?" Rylan asked, plainly confused. "What if she only told you she drugged the soldiers? What if it's a trap?" He looked around at the gathering crowd. "Why would the sovereign's daughter help us defeat her own people?"

"I'm sure," Brice answered, his face becoming serious. "I would trust Roslin with my life." Brice smiled to himself when he realized it was true. "Roslin spent the last few weeks in my camp and has come to view slavery as detestable as we do. Because of her, I've come to understand that not all Ryshtans are the monsters we thought them to be."

One of the men listening to the conversation stepped forward. "Brice speaks the truth," Rogan said. "Lady Roslin asked for my help to drug the wine and deliver it to the soldiers. I personally drove her and the wine to their destination. She risked her life to help us."

Cora stepped forward, too. "It was Lady Roslin who brought me my granddaughter and warned us to run so that her father couldn't use us as a shield against Brice's army. I see no reason to doubt her sincerity."

Brice wrapped his arms around Cora. "It's good to see you." He looked around at the faces of his family, then made eye contact with Dover and smiled. "All of you. I've missed you so much." His face became serious again as he looked at his brothers. "I need you to poll everyone and see who's willing to fight. I'm hoping it won't come to that. There's a chance they'll surrender to our greater number. When Glen gets here, join your forces with his and explain what has happened."

"Won't you be with us?" Collin asked.

"No, I'm going back to Darius. I need to make sure that Roslin made it safely into hiding." Although Brice knew he had been able to move more stealthily without her, he couldn't help wishing now that he had brought Roslin with him. He had a bad feeling and knew it would not ease up until he went back to check.

"When they get here, I want you to surround the palace wall, let them see the reality of our numbers. Even if the soldiers had not been drugged, they would have been hard-pressed to beat us. If you don't hear from me when you get there, assume that I've been incapacitated and Glen will be in charge." With those words, Brice turned and slipped into the darkness.

Athol walked into Roslin's chamber and dumped his unconscious daughter unceremoniously on the bed. Pacing back and forth, he waited for her to come to. He wanted her awake and fully aware of what was happening to her. Growing tired of waiting when it appeared she would not awaken anytime soon, he slapped her a few times until she came around.

Roslin started awake and fought to clear the fogginess in her head. "Get up!" a voice shouted at her, and she opened her eyes to see her father standing at the foot of her bed.

She didn't move fast enough for him, and he grabbed her feet and dragged her off the bed. *This can't be happening*, she thought, as Athol stripped the fine clothes off her body and forced her to put on the simple garments she had been wearing when she arrived home.

As far as Athol was concerned, she was no longer his daughter. She had defected to the other side and would die without honor, dressed in the disgusting rags that would let everyone see the reduction in her station.

Roslin grimaced as her hands were tied tightly behind her and she was dragged from the room. Her brothers Kyle and Lon met them in the hallway and ten-year-old Kyle gasped at the sight of his battered sister. He ran to her, wrapped his arms around her, and burst into tears.

"What happened to you?" he asked, still clinging to her.

Athol pulled Kyle away. There was no keeping what Roslin had done a secret. He decided that now was as good a time as any for them to learn the truth about their traitorous sister. He didn't believe in coddling his children. "With the help of your sister, the slaves have mounted a rebellion. She has doomed us all to be butchered by those ungrateful lowlifes."

Roslin glared at her father. "Ungrateful? Were they supposed to be grateful to you for keeping them as slaves and dehumanizing them?" Roslin took a step closer to Athol, never losing eye contact. "I believed you, Father, when you told me that slaves were so ignorant and lazy they would have died if they hadn't been taken under our control." Roslin looked over to her brothers and continued. "I found them to be just the opposite. They were good, hard-working, caring people. They saved my life and took care of me."

"And they branded you a slave," Athol spat at her.

"Only after Brice found out I had lied to him. That was the day I ran away. The rest of my time with them I was shown nothing but kindness. Not because I was someone important and they feared reprisal. I was a stranger to them, but they took me in and shared what they had with me. What I went through that last day opened my eyes to what we have done to these people. When I think that I participated, it sickens me."

"I can't believe my daughter could turn her back on her family and her people, condemning them to death after such a short time with those barbarians."

Roslin could see that her words were having no effect on her father, but she hoped she could reach her brothers. If for some reason, the Ryshtans managed to win this conflict, her brothers were the future and needed to see the truth. She let her gaze move from one to the other, beseeching them with her eyes. "I'm not a traitor. I'm trying to save our people and theirs. There's no reason we can't all live together as free people."

Athol gripped Roslin's jaw, forcing her to look at him. "And in this free society of yours, who will do the labor? If we don't force them, they won't do anything."

Roslin's eyes bore into her father's, refusing to be intimidated. "You don't have to force them. Just pay them a fair wage or a share in the crops."

"This is ridiculous. If you really think something like that can work, you are crazy. You committed an act of treason by betraying us to the enemy. For that, you will die." He looked at Lon. "This is why women can't be allowed to think for themselves. They have no common sense. Remember that if you live to have your own household." Athol pushed Roslin ahead of him down the hallway, and Kyle started crying again. "Lon, take your brother to his chamber and keep him there."

"Yes, Father," the fifteen-year-old answered. He grabbed his brother's hand and pulled him toward his bedchamber. "Roslin must be mad to talk back to him like that."

Kyle pulled away and ran after his father. "Please don't hurt—" A hand was clapped over his mouth, and he struggled to pull it away.

"If Father says Roslin has to die, so be it. She betrayed us all. It's just punishment."

Roslin was grateful her brothers would not be forced to witness her execution. Kyle had grown especially close to her the last three years. Because of their mother's illness, he had depended on her for the mothering that the ill woman was unable to give. As a female child, she had spent little time with her brothers until then. Girls and boys were schooled separately, and seldom, if ever, were allowed to play together. They were together at mealtime, and that was it.

Roslin noticed that in Brice's camp, girls and boys were schooled together and played together. If Ryshtan boys had not interacted with their mothers, they would have had very little contact with females at all until they were twelve and allowed to take their first bed slave.

Athol pushed her through the door for the walk to the wall surrounding the palace grounds. He planned to hang her in full view of Brice's army as they advanced.

"Lord Athol, they're coming," Captain Alban said, rushing to his sovereign's side.

"How long before they get here?"

"Perhaps five minutes."

Athol pushed Roslin to walk faster; this had to be finished before the rebels reached the wall. "Sorry you won't get to say goodbye to your lover, but you'll be dead before he arrives."

When they reached the steps leading to the sentry walk atop the wall, Roslin stopped. "Please...Father, don't do this. Lay down your arms and talk to them. This can be settled without bloodshed."

Athol stepped around her and dragged her up the stairs. When they reached the walkway, he placed a rope around her neck, then forced her to climb to the edge of the wall. The rope hung down her back, and she could feel it with her fingers. Roslin grasped the rope as her father pushed her off the wall, but when she reached the end of the slack, her arms were wrenched back painfully, causing her to let go. But she had managed to break her fall and prevent her neck from being broken. The weight of her body pulled the knot tight, and she began to strangle.

Brice found the hidden room empty, and panic filled his heart. Something had gone wrong; Roslin had promised she would come here and wait. He vaulted out of the underground room and ran toward the palace grounds. If Lord Athol had already discovered Roslin's efforts to help the slaves, her life would surely be forfeited. Reaching the wall, he climbed it quickly and was horrified to witness Athol push Roslin over the side with a rope around her neck. They were only a hundred feet away, but with Roslin hanging at the end of a rope, it seemed an enormous distance.

Brice did not attempt to catch Roslin's cowardly father as he attempted to escape. His only thought was getting to Roslin in time. If the fall had not broken her neck, she could still be alive. Grasping the rope, he pulled the young woman up until he could reach her shoulders and lift her over the side of the wall.

As Roslin continued to strangle, her vision seemed to be shrinking, like she was looking through a black tunnel that kept getting smaller. Soon the blackness would be complete, and it would be over. She felt hands gripping under her arms and pulling, but the rope around her neck did not loosen. She thought she could hear Brice's voice off in the distance calling her as the darkness finally closed in around her.

Brice lifted Roslin over the wall and removed the rope. He leaned close and could hear her take a gasping breath and pulled her into his arms. His joy was short-lived when he felt a searing pain and looked down to see the tip of an arrow sticking out of his left shoulder. He released Roslin and jumped to his feet, whirling around as he did so. Lord Athol was hiding behind a soldier who sent another arrow flying toward him. It caught Brice in the side, and he momentarily went down on one knee. Rising, he grabbed his sword and stood over Roslin to protect her.

He heard the shouts as his army approached the walls and knew if he could last another minute or two, Roslin would be safe. He couldn't understand how Glen had gotten there so quickly but was grateful that help had arrived in time to save Roslin.

Brice watched the soldier notch another arrow and take aim. Under other circumstances, he would not allow himself to be used for target practice, but he couldn't jump away and leave Roslin unprotected.

"Coward!" he yelled. "Are you afraid to come out from behind your shield and fight me like a man? You disgust me."

Lord Athol pushed the bow down just as the arrow was released. The arrow went low, piercing Brice's thigh.

"No more, he's mine," Athol said. He grabbed Alban's sword and advanced on Brice, a large grin spreading across his face.

Brice stepped forward awkwardly to meet the attack. Pain wracked his body, and he was losing a lot of blood. He gripped his sword tightly and swung with all his might. He had to take Lord Athol down quickly while he still had the strength to fight.

Lord Athol moved in and out as he pressed his attack, and with each blow, Brice could feel himself weakening. When Athol kicked his wounded thigh, the leg buckled and Brice went down hard, gasping for breath. "Revenge is sweet," Athol said, as he stood over Brice, ready to strike the fatal blow.

Dazed and confused, Roslin regained consciousness. As she fought to clear her head, she was horrified to see three arrows protruding from Brice's body. Her father was fighting with him, and Roslin scrambled to her feet as the rebel leader was kicked in the leg and fell. Her father stood over Brice, poised to thrust his blade through her fallen savior. "No!" she screamed, as she ran at her father, hitting him as hard as she could with her shoulder. The unexpected blow sent him sprawling over the edge of the walkway to the ground below.

Roslin watched in horror as her father fell over the edge. She had only wanted to stop him…not kill him. She dropped to her knees, fresh tears making their way down her cheeks. He had not been a loving father, but she had loved him in spite of it. Even though he had tried to kill her, she did not wish him dead. Her heart ached at the taking of a life, but she knew with certainty she would do it again if she had to, to save Brice.

Roslin turned back to the fallen rebel leader. She wished she could reach out and touch him, but her hands were still tied behind her back. Brice looked so pale, and there was so much blood that she began to panic. They were alone on top of the wall now. Alban had fled when he saw that Lord Athol was dead.

Roslin stood and searched the mass of men below, looking for Glen. She was frantic to get someone up there to take care of Brice. She couldn't see Glen, so she yelled for assistance. "Someone please help!" she shouted, as her eyes continued to scan the crowd. "Brice has been injured...he needs help! Please hurry!" She saw Glen push his way through the crowd and rush toward the gate followed closely by three men.

The gate was locked, and Glen immediately scaled the wall. He yelled for others to climb over, as well, to unlock the gate.

Now that she knew help was on the way, Roslin knelt by Brice's side. "Hold on," she said, tears spilling down her face. Roslin's chin trembled and she leaned forward to rest her face on Brice's good shoulder, unable to hold back the wracking sobs any longer.

Brice reached up and stroked her hair. "Don't cry. I'll be all right."

"But there's so much blood," Roslin sobbed, not consoled by Brice's comforting words.

Glen arrived and knelt on the other side of Brice. "I can't leave you alone for a minute or you get yourself in trouble."

Brice tried to shrug and winced. "I wasn't expecting you for a few hours yet. How did you get here so quickly?"

"I left a small escort for the women, children, and wounded. The rest of us mounted up to get here as fast as possible."

Collin, Rylan, and Dover arrived, and Dover dropped to his knees, long-repressed guilt showing plainly on his face. "Brice...I...I'm so sorry."

Brice reached out and took his hand. "It's forgotten."

"But—" Dover tried to speak again, but Brice cut him off.

"I said it was forgotten. I meant it."

Dover looked down at Brice and nodded. The subject was closed, at least for now. "We need to find you a healer."

"Mother can take care of me."

Glen shook his head. "Dover's right. You need a healer now. Mother won't be here for hours." He looked at Roslin. "Is there a healer at the palace?" Roslin nodded, and Glen noticed that her hands were bound behind her back. He pulled out his knife and cut them free.

The four brothers picked Brice up and looked to Roslin for direction. "Where to?" Glen asked.

Roslin rubbed her wrists and hands, trying to take away the numbness the tight leather tie had caused. "I'm going to run ahead and find the healer. When you get to the palace, take Brice up the stairs to my chamber. It's the last door on the right. I'll bring the healer as soon as I find him."

She dashed ahead, hoping that Belvin had not gone into hiding as it seemed all the palace guards had done. With the appearance of Brice's army and the death of their sovereign, all sign of the royal guard had vanished. It was as if they had ceased to exist.

Verda Foster

Chapter 7

Roslin found the healer's chamber in disarray. It looked as though he had quickly gone through his belongings and remedies, taking what was important and leaving the rest. Her panic grew as she realized she had no idea where else to look. She knew with his great bulk he would not be moving fast, so there was hope. If only Shea was here, she could help, but it would be hours before she arrived.

Turning to leave, Roslin stopped dead in her tracks. She was sure she heard a noise coming from the closet. Crossing the room, she listened at the door. Cautiously, she opened it to find Belvin and his belongings packed tightly inside.

The fear on Belvin's face momentarily relaxed into relief as he saw that it was Roslin who had discovered him and not the rebels. His expression became grim again as he noticed her bruised and bleeding face. Extricating himself from the tight confines of the closet, he shouldered his bag and started for the door. "Come, Lady Roslin, we must flee the city before it's overrun by the rebel slaves. No Ryshtan is safe here anymore. The guards have abandoned us to them."

"We're in no danger; they mean us no harm," Roslin said, stepping into the doorway to block his exit.

"No harm?" He looked at her frantically. "I saw the royal guard as they deserted the palace. I called to them to ask what had happened." He gripped Roslin's shoulders. "I'm sorry to have to tell you this, but the rebels have killed your father." Moving her out of the way, he pushed through the door and started down the hall. "The guards took your brothers with them. They should have taken you, too. I'll protect you as best I can, but I'm a healer, not a soldier. Our best chance is to get out of the city and hide."

Roslin grabbed his arm and tried to pull him to a stop, but the large man kept walking. She could plainly see he was scared to death. There was no way she could force this hulking man to come with her, so she decided on another plan of action. "Please come with me to my chamber while I gather a few belongings." She looked up into his eyes. "I'm afraid to go alone, but I'll feel safe if you're with me."

Belvin hesitated for only a moment. The beautiful young woman's words stroked his ego. Nodding at Roslin, he started walking toward the back staircase. "I'll help you, Lady Roslin, but we must be quick."

Glen opened the door and stepped aside to allow his brothers to carry Brice into Roslin's room. They placed him gently on the large canopied bed. They had no more than put him down when the door opened and Roslin entered, followed by a large man. Belvin took one look at the men and turned to run.

Roslin again grabbed his arm to stop him, but the results were the same as before. He continued down the long hallway as if she was not holding onto him at all. "Wait!" Roslin called to the frightened man. "Please, we need your help. They won't hurt you."

Brice's four brothers took chase as the healer lumbered down the hall, catching up easily and surrounding him. It was clear the man was frightened, and they kept their distance for fear he might hurt Roslin in his panic.

"Our brother has been injured and is in need of a healer," Glen said as he took a step closer. He held up his hands to show that he carried no weapons. "I promise no harm will come to you if you help us."

"Why should I believe you?" Belvin gestured toward Roslin. "Look what your people did to Lady Roslin."

"No, they didn't do this. My father did."

Belvin knew Lord Athol's temper. He had in fact experienced it on more than one occasion. Was it possible that Lady Roslin was telling the truth? Realizing that the battle was lost and he really had no choice, he nodded and walked back toward Roslin's chamber. It certainly would do no harm to minister to the injured man, and it might save his life.

"I'm going to need someone to fetch a few things from my chamber," Belvin said.

"Anything you need," Glen answered.

Belvin listed the necessary supplies, and Roslin showed Glen the way. It only took a few minutes and they were back, placing the requested items on the table by the bed.

Belvin nodded his thanks and rummaged through the powders until he found what he was looking for. He placed a few pinches in some water and offered it to Brice. "Drink this," he said.

Brice managed a few good swallows before the strain of trying to sit up became too much, and he was forced to lie back down. He looked at his brothers and smiled. "It's so good to have the family back together after all these years." He squeezed Roslin's hand. "This isn't exactly how I wanted you to meet my brothers for the first time."

Roslin returned the squeeze and Brice felt her hand tremble.

"Don't worry," he said. "I'll be fine as long as you're here."

He struggled to keep his eyes open.

Roslin lifted his hand and pressed her lips into his palm. "Sleep now. I'll be here when you wake up. I promise." She leaned over and gently touched her lips to Brice's forehead.

Brice nodded, as the world slipped away.

Belvin watched Roslin lean over and kiss his patient. "Is he the reason your father beat you so?"

"Part of it."

Belvin nodded and opened his bag. He removed a knife and began to cut his patient's shirt from his body.

When the shirt was removed, Belvin found that the rebel leader's chest was wrapped in a bandage. He wondered if Brice had other injuries that needed tending. He shrugged. Old injuries could wait. He went to work on the more urgent sites, cutting through the pants leg to expose Brice's thigh. The powder had done its work, and Brice slept through the removal of the arrows from his body. Roslin clung to Brice's hand and watched in silence as the healer cleaned and dressed each wound.

"Will he be all right?" she asked, as Belvin finished.

"I think so, as long as infection doesn't set in." He picked up his knife again. "Now let's get these old bandages off and see if new ones are needed."

Roslin remembered the second night she had been in Brice's camp. Shea had insisted on dressing a wound that the rebel leader had told her was just a scratch. Could that be what this was? She shook her head. No, that was too long ago for bandages to still be needed. She watched the healer cut through the layers of cloth. She gasped as the wrapping was removed to reveal the unmistakable breasts of a woman.

Releasing Brice's hand, she backed away from the bed, unable to keep herself from staring at the evidence that Brice had also lied. Turning, she ran from the room and out of the palace, not stopping until she reached the spot in the garden where she had asked Brice for forgiveness. Dropping to her knees, Roslin had only to close her eyes for the vision of Brice's breasts to engulf her again. Anger flooded through her. *He...she...lied to me.* She remembered again how her dishonesty had angered Brice. He had made it clear that because they had grown to love each other there should be no lies between them, yet he had continued to perpetrate a lie while chastising Roslin for hers. Roslin was not sure she could get past the lack of trust that Brice had in her. He had expected Roslin to trust him completely with her secrets, yet trust should work both ways.

Glen saw Roslin run away and could tell she was upset. He rushed to Brice's side, fearing the worst. He found the healer staring at Brice's uncovered chest in disbelief. He walked over and covered Brice, then turned to Belvin. "Is your work finished here?" he asked.

Belvin nodded. "I've done all I can. Your sister's lost a lot of blood, and—"

Glen grabbed the healer's arm and spun him around. "Brice is my brother. You'll do well to remember that." Glen had spent most of his life calling Brice brother, and to tell the truth, to him, that's what Brice was. Now that Roslin and the healer knew, it wouldn't be long before everyone did. It was bound to come out sometime, and Glen was amazed that no one had discovered the secret sooner.

Belvin nodded mutely, then continued. "There will be pain, but no vital inner organs were damaged. He should be up in a few days unless infection sets in." The healer turned to the water basin and washed, then dried his hands. "He'll need to take it easy for two or three weeks, but I don't anticipate any lasting results of these injuries beyond the unavoidable scarring."

"Thank you for taking care of him. We appreciate all you've done."

"Yes…well…I'll be back to check on him a little later. He should sleep until morning." Belvin turned and started for the door. He was relieved that the rebels needed him. He would be safe until they no longer required his services. He was rather expecting an escort waiting to take him to his chambers and was pleasantly surprised to find none. Apparently, he was free to come and go as long as he continued to do their bidding.

Roslin hardly remembered walking back to the palace and up to her mother's bedchamber. The exhaustion of two days without sleep was catching up to her. Collapsing on the bed, she hoped sleep would claim her quickly. Sleep would be the only thing that would stop the vision of Brice's breasts from returning to haunt her. She had known that Brice was not like other men, had even tried to identify what it was about him that didn't quite fit. Now she understood, but this understanding did not seem to make the attraction any less. In fact, it was just the opposite. The sight of those breasts on Brice's strong muscular body somehow seemed to increase the desire she felt.

Brice awoke to pain. It seemed that everything hurt. Opening his eyes, he found himself alone. The first rays of dawn's light were beginning to filter through the windows. He was not accustomed to sleeping in a bed that was long enough for his tall frame, and he wondered why someone of Roslin's stature would have such a bed. Pain could not stop the smile that warmed his features at the thought of her. Roslin had almost given up her life to protect the slaves of Darius and had been willing to forfeit her own father's life to save Brice. It saddened him to think of what she must be going through now, and the smile faded. Roslin must be suffering terrible guilt at having been forced to kill her own father. *I've got to find her, make sure she's all right.* Pushing the covers away, he realized for the first time that the familiar binding he always wore to conceal his breasts was missing. Panic filled his heart. Roslin had said she would stay. That she would be here when he woke up. Had she been repulsed when she found out Brice was a woman? Why else would she not be here as she had promised?

The sound of the door opening brought him out of his musings, and he looked hopefully at the door. Disappointment washed over him when he saw that it was the healer and not Roslin.

"Ah, I see you're awake. How are you feeling this morning?" Belvin asked, as he padded across the room.

"Fine," Brice answered, turning his gaze to the ceiling. He stifled a groan as the healer prodded him to check his progress.

"The pain will start to ease up a bit in a day or two," Belvin said, noting his patient's clenched jaw. "Everything looks good. No sign of infection."

"Do you know where Lady Roslin is?" Brice asked, his eyes tracking to the large man's face.

"She has taken up residence in the sovereign's chamber. I assume she's there now." Belvin saw the fear in Brice's eyes, and he remembered the young woman's reaction the previous evening when she fled the room. He patted Brice's hand. "She's probably still asleep. I'm sure she'll be by to see you later." He hoped the rebel leader would not see the doubt in his eyes.

Turning away, Brice nodded.

The healer was relieved when the door opened and an older woman walked in with a small girl in tow. He excused himself as the child called out and dashed across the floor.

"Papa!" Cadie shouted, running to the bed and crawling into Brice's arms. "They hurt you," she sobbed, burying her face in his neck.

Brice flinched but held on tightly. "Shh, don't cry." He kissed the top of Cadie's head. "I'm going to be fine, little one." He lifted the small face and wiped away the tears.

"You promise?"

"I promise."

Shea sat at the edge of the bed and watched the two embrace. She gave them a moment more of closeness before pulling the child off Brice. "You need to be careful, Cadie, or you'll hurt your papa. No more big hugs until those wounds heal."

Cadie raised her eyes to Brice's face. "Did I hurt you, Papa?" she asked.

"Just a little," Brice answered. He stroked Cadie's face and smiled. "But it was worth it. I needed that hug."

"Want me to tell you a story and make you feel better?" Cadie asked hopefully.

"I would love a story," Brice answered, watching his little girl's face light up. He closed his eyes and let Cadie's voice lull him back to sleep.

Brice was awakened a few hours later by the arrival of Shea with a cup of warm broth. "I think it's time we get some nourishment into you," she said. "Do you need help sitting up?"

"I'm not helpless, Mother," Brice snapped, wincing as he pulled himself to a sitting position.

"I didn't think you were," Shea scolded, as she placed several pillows behind his back.

"I know...I'm sorry. I guess I'm just not in a very good mood right now." He leaned back into the pillows and accepted the mug. His hands were shaking, and Shea reached over to steady them while Brice drank. "Thank you for putting up with me, Mother."

Glen entered the room to find Brice looking much better than the last time he'd checked on him. "Well, back in the land of the living, I see."

Brice's expression sobered. "What's the status in Darius?"

"We've confiscated all the weapons we could find, and all the regular soldiers have been detained. The royal guard and a few of the Ryshtans have gone into hiding, but their numbers are so few, I don't think they'll be foolish enough to try anything without the army to back them up. Thanks to Roslin, we were able to walk in with almost no resistance."

"How is Roslin? Have you seen her?"

"Not since she ran out of here last night." Glen sat on the large bed next to his mother. "She hasn't been by to see you today?"

"No," Brice whispered. "She knows the truth about me, Glen. She was here when—"

"I know," Glen said. "She looked pretty upset when she ran out. Give her some time, she'll come around."

Brice nodded and gave him a halfhearted smile. Glen's words had confirmed his worst fears. Roslin had been horrified to find out he was a woman and ran away. That explained why she was not here when he awoke as she promised she would be.

"We're going to have a family reunion celebration as soon as you're up to it," Shea said, trying to change the subject. "I still have grandchildren I've yet to meet." She patted Brice's hand. "We have so much to be thankful for. Our family back together again is something I've prayed for."

"Yes," Brice smiled at her. "We really do have much to be thankful for." Looking again at his brother, he asked, "Glen, will you go back to camp and fetch me some clothes? I need to get dressed and get out of here."

Glen frowned. "Why do you want to leave? The palace is yours now. You led us to victory; you deserve to claim the prize."

"This is Roslin's home. She can have it, I don't want it. This isn't what I was fighting for." Brice lay back and closed his eyes. "I'm tired. I just want to go home."

"You get some rest and we'll be back for you with a litter before you know it," Shea said, leaning down to kiss Brice's pale cheek. "We've got a lot of work to do," she told Glen as they walked to the door.

Glen nodded and started back to camp to pick up Brice's belongings. He promised Shea he would find his brothers and their families and send them over to help her get the old residence cleaned and ready so they could bring Brice home as he'd requested.

Chapter 8

Mid-afternoon found Roslin pacing back and forth in her room. Although she had been exhausted when she went to bed the night before, her troubled mind would not let sleep take her until almost daybreak. She had spent her sleepless night pondering her feelings for Brice and had come to the conclusion that she loved him with all her heart. But she was still hurt and angry that he had not trusted her with his secret and decided it was time to confront Brice. If they were to have a deep committed relationship, they had to trust each other.

Her mind made up, she walked to her bedchamber, only to find it empty. Her heart stopped. What could this mean? When she left Brice the night before, he was in no condition to go anywhere. Why hadn't anyone told her that something had happened to him? She ran outside and stopped the first person she saw.

"Please…can you tell me what happened to Brice?"

"His brothers came for him about an hour ago, said they were taking him home."

Roslin's heartbeat slowly returned to normal as it sank in that death had not claimed her love in the night as she had feared. It puzzled her that Brice's family would take him away from the healer and the comforts of the palace. She hurried toward the palace gates, sure she could get someone to direct her to Brice's home once she was in the village.

As Roslin walked through what used to be the slave village, the former slaves were happy to point her in the right direction. Word of her deeds had spread quickly, and they were all grateful for the help she had given their people.

"Welcome to my home," Shea said as she held the door open for Roslin to enter. "I was hoping you would come."

"I need to see Brice."

Shea nodded. She could see the anger in the young woman's eyes and her heart sank. Brice had already been through so much. Losing Roslin would be hard for him to bear. "Before you do, I need to tell you my part in all this. Perhaps when you know the truth, you won't feel such anger toward Brice."

Shea walked slowly to her kitchen table and sat down. "Sit, child, and I'll try to explain."

Roslin sat across from Shea and folded her arms on the table. Shea had been good to her. She could at least listen to what she had to say.

Shea reached over and squeezed Roslin's hand and looked into her eyes. "I mean no disrespect to you, but your grandfather was a monster. We had all heard the horror stories about Lord Galen and his bed slaves. The lucky ones died quickly."

Roslin dropped her eyes to the table, unable to maintain eye contact. Her grandfather, Lord Galen, died when she was six years old, and she had no strong memories of him. Her heart ached when she thought of the pain her family had caused these people. "I have no reason to doubt that what you say is true," she said, her gaze returning to Shea's face. "But what does this have to do with Brice?"

"My husband bred and trained Governor Gage's racing stock. They were the finest in Ryshta, and after the sovereign's horses suffered one too many defeats, Lord Galen demanded that Governor Gage send his two finest horses and his master trainer as part of your mother's dowry."

"You were a dowry gift?"

Shea nodded. "It was the summer before Brice turned five, and he had not yet been counted."

"Counted?"

"Our children were not counted by the Ryshtans until they reached the age of five. At that time, they were branded and added into the master's inventory of slaves."

Roslin's hand involuntarily went to her arm and she shuddered at the image of all those small children being held down and branded. "I hadn't realized they branded such young children." She squeezed her eyes shut, and a tear made its way down her face. "How could we do that to such babes?" She shook her head. "How could we do that to anyone?"

Shea took a cloth from her pocket and handed it to Roslin to dry her tear-stained face. "That's something I've never been able to understand, child, but it's been our lives for as long as I can remember. When we were told we had been given to Lord Galen, I thought my heart would stop. Parents had been known to murder their own daughters to save them from him."

Shea ran her fingers through her salt and pepper hair and continued. "As I said before, Brice had not yet been counted. It was easy for us to start over in Darius with five sons, instead of four sons and a daughter. No one knew us here. No one questioned our deception."

"But how could you teach such a small child to pretend she was a boy?"

"Brice wasn't like other girls. When he was only three years old, he told me he was a boy. I gave little thought to it at the time and attributed it to the fact that he had four older brothers to identify with. It was more difficult to make sure the older boys didn't slip and say they had a sister. It wasn't long before we all accepted Brice as the youngest son in our family."

The family had finally stopped fussing over him, and Brice was alone at last. Everything had gone much better than he had ever imagined. They had defeated the sovereign and with almost no bloodshed. He knew he should be elated, but without Roslin at his side, the victory was a hollow one.

He heard a knock at the door. "Come," he called, turning to see who it was. The door opened, and there in the doorway stood the most beautiful vision he had ever seen. A smile crept across his face. "I was hoping you would come."

Roslin walked to the bedside chair and sat. She looked around the small room and wondered at Brice's decision to leave the palace and come here. "How are you feeling today?"

"Good," Brice lied. Roslin's eyes burned into him, and he knew she could see the truth.

"You look awful," Roslin said, scooting her chair closer.

"Okay, I hurt. But after seeing you, I feel so much better. You're just the medicine I needed."

"Brice…" Roslin paused, not sure how to broach the subject of truth and commitment.

"Yes…?" Brice answered, suddenly afraid.

"I…" Another pause. "I need to talk to you, but perhaps it needs to wait until you're stronger."

Now Brice was really frightened. He was sure that Roslin meant to tell him she didn't love him anymore but wanted to wait until he recovered to give him the bad news.

Brice's face became hard. "If you're going to tell me you don't want me, do it now. I don't need to lie here wondering."

"No, I wanted to talk to you about how hurt I was that you didn't trust me enough to tell me the truth. You were furious at me for keeping the truth about me a secret, and all the time you were keeping your own secret. Do you realize what a hypocrite that makes you?"

"It's not the same thing," Brice answered defensively.

"How is it different?" Roslin asked, letting her anger surface again.

"The difference is, I had every intention of telling you. When I found myself falling in love with you, I wanted to tell you. In fact, that's what I'd started to tell you the day I discovered your secret. Would you have ever told me the truth if I had not found out on my own?"

Roslin thought for a moment. She wanted to believe that she would have eventually, but she wasn't sure. "I really don't know." She reached over and squeezed his hand. "I hated lying to you, Brice, but when it started, I was afraid, and by the time I was certain I didn't need to fear you, it was too late. I didn't know how to tell you. I was afraid of losing you."

"And how do you feel about me now?" Brice asked, his grip tightening on her hand.

"I love you," Roslin answered without hesitation. "But I need to know that I can trust you, that we can trust each other. It works both ways."

"Yes...both ways. Can we put the lies behind us and start over?"

In answer, Roslin leaned over and kissed him gently on the lips.

Brice awoke to find Roslin asleep in the chair, her head resting on the bed. He stroked her hair and smiled. She was still here. Everything was going to be all right. He turned on his side and stifled a groan as pain shot through his body.

Roslin started awake. "Are you all right?" she asked, sitting upright and taking Brice's hand.

Brice smiled to reassure her. "I'm fine, just moved the wrong way." He cupped Roslin's cheek. "You should've gone home to your bed. You're going to be as stiff and sore as I am sleeping bent over my bed like that."

"I don't want to leave you. I'm your best medicine, remember?" She brought her hand up to cover the large hand caressing her cheek.

Brice nodded. "The only medicine I need."

"If you want me to go home, you'll have to come with me. I have no intention of being separated from you again."

Brice couldn't help the silly grin that spread across his face. He had no desire to live at the palace, but now the thought of sharing his life with Roslin made any objections he may have had vanish. It was his lady's home and he would not take that from her. He could not deny that the thought of sharing that large bed with her was also appealing. "My brothers are going to get tired of moving me back and forth."

"Well, we don't want to upset your brothers, so I guess you'll have to stay here."

"Oh, no. You're going home, and I'm coming with you. They'll survive." Brice pulled Roslin down for a kiss and winced as his muscles complained at the effort. Ignoring it, he deepened the kiss.

Roslin felt Brice's body tense for a moment, then relax again. She pulled away and stood up. "Uh-uh, no more of that until those wounds heal. I want you to rest like a good little girl."

Brice reacted immediately. "Don't ever call me that!" he said sharply. "I am not a girl! I never have been, and I don't intend to start now."

"I'm…sorry," Roslin stammered, "I didn't mean…"

Brice saw the stricken look on Roslin's face and wished he could take the words back. "No, you don't need to apologize. You didn't do anything wrong. I'm sorry I snapped at you like that." Brice's eyes pleaded with her to understand. "I'm…uncomfortable being referred to as a girl, and I should've just explained that to you instead of biting your head off."

Roslin smiled. "I promise I'll never call you a girl again." She walked back to the bed and sat down, her expression thoughtful. "I would never knowingly say something that would make you uncomfortable." She paused a moment. "You do believe that, don't you?"

Brice pulled himself up into a sitting position. "Yes, I do." He let his hand slide up Roslin's arm, stroking gently. "With all my heart." His hand stilled when he felt Roslin flinch. He lifted her sleeve and shook his head at the site of the raw brand mark. "I'll never forgive myself for doing that to you."

"I wish you would. I've forgiven you, and that whole experience taught me a valuable lesson. You gave me a small taste of what it was like to be a slave, and it helped me understand what your people have had to endure their whole lives." Roslin cupped Brice's face and brushed her thumb across his lips. "As unpleasant as it was, I think I needed that."

"No one needs to be tortured and humiliated," Brice said sadly.

Roslin smiled. "And thanks to you, no one will have to suffer that fate again." She leaned over and kissed him. "I'm very proud of you." She stood and started for the door. "Now I'm going to go find someone to help me take you home," she called over her shoulder, and was gone.

Brice lay back and smiled. *Home...She wants to make a home with me.* All was right with the world.

Chapter 9

"How much pork drippings did you put in?" Roslin asked Shea, as she sat at the table watching the older woman make cornbread. She was writing the instructions down, so she could remember later.

"Oh, I don't know, I guess about the size of an egg." Shea reached for the milk pitcher and started pouring milk in a little at a time, stirring as she did so.

"How can you just pour milk from the pitcher like that?" Roslin asked, puzzled. "If you don't measure, how do you know when you have enough?"

"Well, you just pour a little and stir, then pour some more. Keep doing that until it won't peak."

"What does 'won't peak' mean?" Roslin asked, her confusion growing. This learning to cook thing was complicated.

Shea crooked her finger at the young woman. "Come closer and I'll show you."

Roslin walked around to the other side of the table and looked into the bowl of thick batter. Shea lifted the spoon out several times, leaving small peaks that looked like a range of jagged mountains. "See how the batter is thick and stands up in these little peaks?" Roslin nodded, and Shea stirred a little more milk, then lifted the spoon again. She still had peaks, but they did not stand up as high. A little more milk was added, and the batter would not hold a peak. "There, you see?

Now we have enough milk." She smiled at Roslin and patted her cheek. Turning to Cadie, the older woman asked, "Did you get that pan greased, little one?"

Cadie nodded. "All done."

"Good girl, you're such a big help."

Cadie grinned from ear to ear at the compliment, as Roslin pulled her into her lap, tickling the child. "When I'm able to do this cooking stuff by myself, you can be my number one helper, and your papa will be so proud of us."

The kitchen rang with the sound of laughter.

Belvin replaced the dressing on Brice's wounds. "They look really good, we got lucky. Infection can be very nasty when it sets in." He sat down in the large chair by the bed. "I hope you believe I didn't mean to expose your secret to Lady Roslin. I…I didn't know."

"No one knew except my family." Brice paused a moment. "Have you told anyone?"

"I would never betray a secret of one of my patients," Belvin replied sincerely. "You may not believe me, but I'm glad you defeated the sovereign. I was afraid at first; I thought your people would take out your just revenge on all of us." He looked down at his hands, sighing deeply. "I have never agreed with slavery. Lady Roslin can attest to the fact that I owned no slaves, but…" His gaze lifted again. "I'm ashamed to say that I was afraid to speak out against it. I was a coward. Many of us were."

"That's in the past. We're all starting over with a clean slate." Brice extended his hand. "I would be proud to call you friend." He wondered how many more Ryshtans were just like Belvin—not agreeing with slavery but afraid to speak out for fear of what the sovereign would do to them. Knowing Roslin and the healer made him realize that his prejudice against all Ryshtans had been wrong.

Belvin smiled and grasped Brice's hand firmly. They looked up to see Roslin walking in the door with a tray laden with foodstuffs, followed closely by Shea and Cadie. "Well, I will leave you to your family," the large man said, nodding his goodbye to the new arrivals. "Ladies."

Cadie ran across the floor. "Papa, we brought you some stew and cornbread." She pointed to the tray Roslin was setting on the bedside table. "Gram made it, but Roslin and I helped."

"If you two helped, then it has to be wonderful." Brice sat up and extended his good arm, giving the child a one-armed hug. Embracing his daughter was a bit painful, but the girl needed to see that Brice was all right. A little pain was worth it. Releasing the child, Brice got to his feet.

"Ah, ah, ah..." Roslin said, blocking his path. "Whatever you need, I'll get. You climb right back in bed."

"All right," Brice said obligingly. "If you would be so kind as to empty my bladder for me, I would be most appreciative."

Roslin grinned and stepped aside. "If I could, I would."

"I know, love," Brice said. He gave Roslin a quick peck on the cheek, then disappeared through the doorway.

Shea watched him leave, then smiled at Roslin. "I don't think I've ever seen Brice so happy. Thank you for that."

"I've never been happier, either. Loving Brice feels as natural as breathing and as necessary." Roslin looked from Shea to Cadie. "Thank you for making me feel welcome in your family."

Roslin thought of her own family. Of the brothers who were lost to her. Now that Brice was out of danger, the need to find them and make sure they were all right had become stronger. She had become Kyle's surrogate mother when he was seven, and she was sure he would want to come and stay with her. She was not as sure about Lon. He had been older when their mother become ill and had not attached himself as firmly to her apron strings. The important thing was to get them back home to Darius as soon as possible, wherever they stayed. She knew they were as lacking in the skills to take care of themselves as she was and hoped that someone was looking after them. Brice had sent out scouting parties to find them, but as yet, they had not been located.

It had been almost four weeks since the liberation of Darius. Brice was pleased that Roslin had finally taken his word that he was fine and stopped treating him like an invalid. There was work to be done and her constant hovering had made that difficult, even though Brice enjoyed the attention.

The people were clamoring for Brice to take on the mantel of sovereign of Ryshta, and he had called a meeting to announce his decision. People had been arriving for some time now, and Brice frowned as he looked over the crowd. He had sent word that there would be a meeting and that all people of Darius were invited, yet he saw not one female face in the large group. In the past, town meetings had been limited to men, and perhaps they had misunderstood the invitation. He stood and strode to the platform that his brother Rylan had built for the occasion. With a nod to Glen, the bells were sounded, signaling time to begin.

All eyes went to the tall figure on the dais, and a hush fell over the crowd. "My friends," Brice began, his strong, full voice carrying easily across the crowd. "I had hoped to see the women of Darius here today. In the future, any town meeting called will include women, as well, or it'll be canceled." Grumbling voices could be heard throughout the crowd at the thought of women taking part in matters of state. Brice lifted his hands to quiet the mutterings and continued. "I've called you here today to explain my plans for the future of Ryshta." He let his gaze sweep the sea of people, making eye contact with as many as possible. He wanted them to feel that he was speaking to each one individually. "You have bestowed on me the title of your sovereign, and although I appreciate the gesture, I cannot accept it."

A rumble started through the crowd, and shouts of, "But you are The Chosen," could be heard. Brice lifted his hands, and the people quieted down again.

"I believe we need to work together to govern ourselves," he continued. "The new government will consist of twelve people, six of whom will be elected by the people, and six, including myself, who I will choose. These six will be appointed for life or until they choose to step down. When a spot becomes vacant in the permanent council, a replacement will be chosen by the entire council."

The murmur in the crowd increased again, and Brice noted that although the people seemed surprised, they did not seem displeased with his decision. "These twelve people will work together to draft a new constitution. This new constitution must be approved by at least two-thirds of the twelve to become law. An election will be held in two months time, and you will choose the six to represent you."

Brice walked to the edge of the stage and extended his hand toward a small group of five people standing to the left. "These are the other five permanent members of our new governing council. My brother Glen, my mother Shea—"

There was an audible gasp that spread through the throng of people. Mikah pushed his way to the front. "We can't have women deciding our future," he spat. "This is ridiculous." He looked at the others waiting to be introduced. "How can you possibly think we could allow Ryshtans on our ruling council?" He nodded at Roslin and Belvin. "We defeated them and now you want them to help rule us?"

"We're all free people now, Mikah." Brice jumped down from the stage to tower over the older man. "Our new government needs to represent all the people, women and Ryshtans included. We need to see the views of all sides to make decisions that are fair to all."

Mikah glared at Brice. "Were the Ryshtans fair to us?"

"Stop talking about the past. It's over. We have to think about the future. We didn't win our freedom only to turn the tables and enslave the slavers." Brice stepped back onto the stage. "I choose these five people for their wisdom and compassion. "You all put your faith in me when you asked me to lead you. This is how I choose to lead, and this decision is final." Brice turned and strode from the stage, his long legs moving him quickly toward the palace.

Roslin broke into a run to follow Brice, catching him as he climbed the palace steps. "Don't let him upset you," she said, taking his hand and squeezing. "The people believe in you; they won't listen to him. After all, you are The Chosen." She stepped in front of Brice, reaching up to wrap her arms around his neck. "And you belong to me."

Brice cocked his head and smiled teasingly. "You think so?"

"Oh, I know so."

Brice took Roslin's hand and pulled her toward the door. "I told Mother I needed some time alone with you. I asked her to keep Cadie for the night." Once inside the door, Brice pulled her close again. "I know it hasn't been easy for you these last few weeks. You've been taking care of me and Cadie and trying to cope with all the changes and confusion." Brice lifted the small hand he still held and pressed it to his lips. "I want to make it up to you." His eyes dropped from Roslin's eyes to her mouth. "Tonight is just for us." He leaned down to kiss her again. "I want to make love to you, but more than that, I want to make a life with you." Brice pulled back and gazed into green eyes overflowing with love. "Will you consent to be my wife?"

"Oh, yes," Roslin answered, wrapping her arms around Brice's neck, pulling him down for another kiss. Their lips met, and this time, the kiss was more urgent.

When the kiss ended, Brice turned and led Roslin up the stairs. The wait was finally over; tonight he would make love with this precious woman.

Brice joined Roslin in the large bed, his heart pounding wildly at the thought that he was finally going to make love to this woman he loved more than his own life. Propping himself up on one elbow, he stroked Roslin's beautiful face with his free hand. "I love you." He bent down and brushed her lips with his own. "I need to touch you," he whispered, slipping his hands under her dress, pushing it up. He smiled at the gasp that escaped Roslin's lips. Now her breasts were exposed, and Brice devoured them with his eyes. Leaning down, he nibbled and suckled at first one breast, then the other.

Roslin's breathing was reduced to short, aching gasps, as she wound her fingers tightly in Brice's hair. "Yes...please, touch me," she begged. A groan escaped her lips when her nipple was pulled into her lover's mouth.

Brice let his hands explore downward until they stopped at Roslin's panties. Grasping the delicate undergarment, he slipped them off. Next he pulled the dress over Roslin's head, then covered the small body with his own, thrusting rhythmically against her. His mouth sought out Roslin's mouth, the kiss urgent and deep. Breaking the kiss, he let his teeth nip their way down her slender throat.

Roslin felt her body exploding with desire, the likes of which she had never experienced before. Her hands clenched and unclenched Brice's hair frantically, and a fleeting thought that she might be hurting him evaporated as her lover continued his sensual assault down her body.

Sliding still farther, Brice nuzzled the soft curly hair at the apex of Roslin's legs. He let his index finger stroke ever so softly along the opening to his lover's need. He settled himself between Roslin's thighs, her scent intoxicating beyond belief. He stroked her with his tongue, holding her tightly when Roslin's bucking hips threatened to dislodge him. He was in ecstasy when Roslin stiffened and his name was raggedly torn from her lips.

Brice waited a moment, then slowly climbed back up Roslin's body, cradling her gently in his arms. He could feel her ragged breathing slowing and returning to normal. He'd been surprised—and pleased—at how passionate Roslin had been. Elsbeth, his only basis for comparison, had always seemed to enjoy his touch but nothing like this. There was no comparison to the desire he had felt emanating from Roslin as he made love to her.

Roslin had no idea that making love could be this wonderful. Her mother had explained to her that she must submit to the young man her father had chosen for her to marry, and in time, if she was lucky, she might grow to love him. But love him or not, if he called her to his bed, she must submit—it was her duty. She understood now that when it is with someone you love, it is beautiful beyond belief. She slipped her hand under Brice's shirt, the need to touch him overpowering. Instantly, a strong hand grabbed her wrist and pulled her hand away.

"I need to touch you, to please you," Roslin said, reaching under the shirt again.

"You have pleased me. More than you can know," he answered, removing the hand again gently, but firmly. "Let's try to get some sleep."

Roslin lay with her head on Brice's shoulder, trying to understand what had just happened. No one had ever affected her this way, and she ached from the need to touch Brice. He had been so gentle and caring when he made love to her but had been very firm that Roslin was not to touch him. He had kept his breasts bound and his clothes on. She knew that it had pleased Brice to make love to her, but the fact that he did not seem to want or desire her touch hurt.

Mikah stood in front of the assembled men in the meeting hall. He had called this meeting of the newly freed men of Darius to make them see the folly of following Brice in this ridiculous new plan for governing themselves. The mere thought of Ryshtans and women making rules and sitting in judgment over the freed men was repugnant to him. He was determined to make them understand.

He had not invited Brice, nor had he invited any of the Ryshtan men, but he had not kept the meeting a secret, either. He supposed it was possible that Brice might show up, but he doubted it. Brice had made it clear that they were free to assemble and campaign.

"Men of Darius," Mikah began. "I know Brice is responsible for the overthrow of the Ryshtan regime, and I'm as grateful as the rest of you to him for my freedom. But does that give him the right to reinstall Ryshtans in a place of power over us?" He paused to let his words sink in. Mikah was no fool. He knew Brice was well loved and respected. He had to be careful with his judgment of the man, or the crowd just might turn on him for attacking their savior.

"It's clear that, through no fault of his own, he has lost his heart to one of them." Mikah continued, "And perhaps she is responsible for the strange decisions he has made. Roslin is not only Ryshtan, she's a woman. Either should be enough to keep her off the governing council. I fear she has bewitched him." Mikah shook his head sadly. "How else can you explain the changes we've seen in him? When Brice left Darius five years ago, he was bent on revenge. There's no way the Brice I knew would've placed one of them in a position of power, yet that's exactly what he has done. He has installed two of them on the permanent board. He can't be in his right mind."

Rogan stood. "I'll fight any man who would say a disparaging word against Lady Roslin." He looked around the room. "Have you forgotten that she is responsible for drugging the solders so Brice's army could march into Darius practically unopposed?" His voice trembled with anger. "She chose us over her own people."

"That's right," someone else shouted. "She carries the brand, she's one of us now."

"She may be one of us, but she's still a woman," Mikah said, lifting his voice to be heard above the murmurs of the crowd. "How many of you feel your women should be allowed to decide how we are governed?" He looked around the room, as the men sat silent, none willing to relinquish his role of authority to a woman. "Decisions on the welfare of our community and our families have always been the responsibility of men." Mikah paced back and forth, his arms moving rapidly to emphasize his words. "Women were given to men to take care of us and bear our children. Not to make decisions that can affect us for the rest of our lives." His pacing stopped, and he faced the crowd. "Follow him if you must, but don't give up control in your own households. If Brice must rule over us, so be it. Your women belong to you, not Brice. You have control…use it."

Mikah took a deep breath and ran a hand through his hair. "I'll run for a place on the governing council. I would hope you'll vote for me, for I will use my vote to make sure that women are kept in their place where they belong."

Applause rang through the room, and Mikah knew he had found a platform that the men of Darius would support.

Shea walked up the main staircase in the palace and headed for Roslin's bedchamber. She had made a quilt and wanted to put it on the bed to surprise Brice. She wanted something made by her own hand in this grand house, so Brice would feel more at home. It was a good time to slip into their bedchamber unnoticed because Roslin was in the kitchen preparing the evening meal, and Cadie had talked her into letting her help. She had been teaching Roslin to cook, and tonight was her first attempt at it on her own. She had asked Shea to leave so she could brag to Brice that she did it herself.

The door was open, and Shea was surprised to see Brice sitting on the large bed. He was unaware of his audience, and his face was clearly troubled. The sound of footsteps caused him to turn to the door, and their eyes met. His expression changed immediately, but he could see in Shea's eyes that it was too late.

"You might as well tell me," Shea said, sitting next to him. "I know something's bothering you." She reached out and patted a large callused hand.

Brice looked up at his mother and shook his head. "Am I really that transparent?"

"I know you better than most."

Brice nodded. "Rogan came to see Roslin today, and he brought her a basket of eggs. Her face lit up when she saw him. She hugged him, and my heart almost pounded out of my chest." Brice fought against the jealous insecurity that had welled up inside of him at the sight. He looked at Shea, fear plainly visible on his face. "I was afraid, Mother. I don't know what I'd do if she ever decided to leave me for a man." Brice shook his head, unable to shake the image. "I can't help but wonder why Roslin wants some poor excuse for a man, when she could have the real thing. I'm sure she wishes I were a real man."

"You think I wish you were a man?" Roslin asked incredulously.

Brice was startled to hear Roslin's voice. He could see anger flare in those beautiful green eyes and wondered how long she had been standing in the doorway. The silence in the room was deafening, as the two stared at each other. Shea silently rose and left the two troubled young people alone to talk.

Roslin walked to where Brice sat and knelt before him. Her anger was replaced by sorrow that Brice could doubt her love. She repeated her question softly and without anger this time. "Do you really believe that I wish you to be anything other than what you are?"

"Elsbeth did. She despised what I am." Brice looked down at his hands, unable to maintain eye contact. "She loved me in her way, but she never wanted me to do anything to remind her that I wasn't what I appeared to be." Brice paused, remembering how desperate his devotion to Elsbeth had been. He would have done anything to keep her in his life.

Roslin reached out and covered Brice's hands with her own. "She never wanted to look at your beautiful body...to touch you?"

The pain shown plainly on his face as Brice brought his eyes up to meet Roslin's gaze. "No...never."

Roslin couldn't believe what she was hearing. Just the mere thought of caressing those beautiful breasts and running her hands over Brice's muscular body made her tingle all over, and she could feel the slick wetness coating her undergarment. She realized now that it was not that Brice did not desire her touch. He was afraid. Afraid that if he did not keep that part of himself hidden, she wouldn't want him anymore.

"I don't want a man, I want you, and I don't want to pretend you're anything other than what you are." Roslin reached up, gently cupping Brice's face in her hands. "You're not some poor excuse for a man; you're magnificent." She let her thumbs brush softly across Brice's lips. "I love the fact that you're a masculine woman. The thought of touching you sends shivers down my spine. I want to...no, I need to...touch you. I desire you. Please don't push me away."

Standing, Roslin pulled Brice's shirt over his head, then knelt again, leaning over to kiss his belly. She felt him tremble at her touch, heard his breath catch. She touched the tightly wound binding around Brice's chest, then looked up questioningly, requesting permission with her eyes to remove this unwelcome barricade.

Brice closed his eyes and lifted his arms to allow Roslin to unwrap the binding. He believed Roslin, yet his stomach clenched as panic filled him. With each layer that was removed, his panic grew. He knew the fear was not rational, but he had no control over it. Opening his eyes, he reached to still his partner's hands from their task.

Roslin looked up and her heart broke when she saw the pain in his eyes. She climbed on the bed and pulled him into her arms. Brice wasn't ready to allow the feminine part of himself to be revealed yet. Perhaps he never would. "It's all right," she cooed as he snuggled close.

"I'm sorry," Brice whispered. "I really wanted to...I'm sorry." Tears started down his face, and he clung desperately to Roslin, as if the young woman would disappear if he let go.

"Shh, it's okay. When the time is right, I'll be here. I'm not going anywhere." Roslin stroked the dark head pressed against her chest, then reached over and grabbed the blanket, pulling it over them. She could feel Brice's body relaxing against her, and she bent down to kiss his head. "I love you."

Brice awoke to find the first rays of sunlight dimly illuminating the room. He could feel Roslin pressed firmly against his back, her arm draped around his waist. They had forgone the evening meal waiting downstairs, silently holding onto each other the night before until sleep claimed them.

Brice slipped out of bed, collecting the cloth wrap that had finished working its way off his chest sometime during the night. He felt a little awkward after his behavior the previous evening and wanted to distance himself from Roslin to think this through. He dressed quickly and made his way downstairs, grabbed a bucket, and started outside to fill it. The sound of footsteps caught his attention, and he turned in the direction of the sound.

"We found them!" Glen called out, running toward him at full tilt.

"Found who?" Brice asked. "Roslin's brothers?"

"Yes," Glen answered excitedly. "A runner arrived this morning with their location. It'll take me about a week to get to where they were last spotted." Glen took a few good breaths, then continued. "Our men are following at a distance and marking the trail for us."

Brice threw his arms around Glen, his face erupting in a huge smile. "Finally, some good news."

Releasing his hold, Brice turned to hurry back to Roslin with the news. "Take plenty of men with you," he shouted over his shoulder. "I want this over with quickly." His awkwardness forgotten, he ran up the stairs, taking them two at a time. He couldn't wait to wake Roslin.

Roslin felt a gentle shaking, and her eyes fluttered open to the beautiful sight of Brice leaning over her with a radiant smile on his face.

"I have wonderful news," Brice said, reaching out to ruffle Roslin's sleep-disheveled hair. "They found your brothers. Glen just told me."

Roslin sat bolt upright in bed, her eyes sparkling with excitement. "When will they be here?"

"Not sure, probably no more than three weeks."

Roslin threw her arms around Brice. At last, her brothers were coming home.

Brice's thoughts drifted to the two boys who would be joining their household. He and Roslin now had three children to raise instead of one. Of course, Lon was practically grown, but Kyle would be with them for some time to come.

This was not something he had bargained for when he fell in love with Roslin, but they were now very much a part of the package. He would deal with them as best he could. After all, he expected Roslin to take on his child; he could do no less.

Chapter 10

"I think I need to tell Cadie first," Brice said to Roslin, as they rode in the gently rocking carriage toward his mother's house.

"Do you think she'll accept me as her mother?" Roslin asked. "I don't want her to think I'm trying to replace Elsbeth in her heart."

Brice pulled the horse to a stop and turned to face Roslin. "I'm sure she has room in there for both of you." He smiled and wrapped his arms around her. "You worry too much. Cadie loves you. Don't you know that by now?"

Turning back to the road, he slapped the reins, causing the carriage to jerk to a start.

The house came into view, and Brice could see Cadie dangling from a rope swing in the side yard. When the little girl caught sight of them, she squealed with glee, releasing the swing and bounding across the yard to greet them.

Shea heard the commotion and popped her head out the door to see what all the fuss was about. "You're just in time for the midday meal."

"Is there anything I can do to help?" Roslin asked, taking Shea's arm and starting for the door. She knew Brice wanted to speak with Cadie alone, and this seemed a good way to leave them to themselves.

"You've gotten pretty good at making gravy," Shea answered. "You work on that, and we'll be just about ready." The two disappeared through the doorway, leaving Brice and Cadie alone in the yard.

Brice sat on a stump and pulled the little girl into his lap. "Are you happy with us living with Roslin?" Brice asked.

Cadie nodded. "I love Roslin."

Brice smiled. "I love her, too. I want us to be a family." He put a finger under the girl's chin, tilting her head up. "I asked Roslin to be my wife, and she said yes."

"Does that mean she'll be my mother?" Cadie asked, a hopeful look on her face.

Brice paused a moment. "Would you like Roslin to be your mother?"

"Oh, yes, Papa, yes," Cadie said, scrambling to her feet on his lap and throwing her arms around Brice's neck, squeezing tightly. Then she jumped down and ran to the door. "Gram, Gram! Roslin's going to be my mother," she called to Shea, as she bounced up and down in the doorway.

The little girl danced across the room and into Roslin's arms. Brice stood in the doorway and watched the grin spread across Roslin's face as she wrapped her arms around her new daughter. The joy she felt at the child's acceptance of her new position in her life was clearly painted in that radiant smile.

Chapter 11

Glen watched as his men took up their positions, surrounding the Ryshtan camp and cutting off any means of escape. He knew how important it was to Roslin to not only bring her brothers back to her, but to do it without shedding any blood.

As the dawn's light slowly made its appearance over the horizon, the Ryshtan guards posted on night watch saw for the first time that an army of men had surrounded them in the night without their knowledge. Sounding the alarm, they took up defensive positions, waiting for Captain Alban to give the order to fight or to surrender to the enemy's overwhelming numbers.

"How did this happen?" Alban shouted, as he ran to join his men. "Were you sleeping at your post?"

"No, sir," the young soldier on watch answered quickly.

"Are we going to surrender, sir?" an inexperienced soldier not much more than a boy asked hopefully.

Alban walked over to the boy and looked him in the eye. "We're dead either way, soldier. Do you really think they're going to let us live?" His eyes swept those of his frightened men. "I say, if we're going to die, we take as many of them with us as we can before we go. What do you say, men? Are you with me?"

"We're with you, sir," came the chant from his men, and together they turned to face the enemy.

Captain Alban was surprised to see one of the rebel slaves step away from the others, toss his sword to the ground, and walk forward, his hands held out to the side.

"I'm unarmed. I mean you no harm." Glen kept his arms away from his body and slowly turned so they could see he carried no weapons. "I have a message to relay from our leader Brice, then you're free to go as you choose."

Alban tossed his sword to the ground and nodded his willingness to talk. He had been certain they were all going to die, but now a ray of hope had been dangled in front of him, and he intended to find out what these people wanted. Holding his arms away from his body as the slave had done, he approached the man cautiously. "What is it Brice wants from us? You have already taken our homes and our livelihood."

Glen watched the man approach and wondered how loyal he was to the sovereign's family, now that Lord Athol was dead. Would he be willing to die to keep Roslin's brothers with him? "We have installed a new order in Ryshta. All people are now free, including you and the people hiding here under your protection. We do not wish to enslave you, as your people have done to us for generations. Slavery has been a blight on this land long enough."

Glen could see the people behind Alban looking at one another in wonder at his words. "It won't be an easy peace, for there is much resentment on both sides, but our leader Brice is determined to make peace work between our people." Glen let his eyes travel from person to person, letting them know he was speaking to each one as an individual. It was something he had learned from Brice to pull the audience to him and gain their confidence. "You're all free to return to Darius or leave as you choose. No one will pursue you for retribution."

"How can you expect us to believe you?" Alban asked, crossing his arms across his chest defiantly.

"Because if we wanted you dead, I would not be here talking to you right now." Glen gestured behind him. "It's obvious we have you outnumbered by at least ten to one. It would've been easy to just ride in and massacre the lot of you."

"So you're just going to turn around and ride back to Darius and leave us be?" This seemed too good to be true. There must be a catch. "You want nothing in return?"

"Lady Roslin has a request. She wishes her brothers to be returned to her. Give them to me, and I'll escort them safely home."

"And if I refuse?"

"Then we'll take them. I wish your people no harm, but I have orders to bring Roslin's brothers to her. I intend to do that, with or without your cooperation."

Alban absentmindedly stroked his beard as he glanced over his shoulder at his solders and the group of high-born Ryshtans who were under their protection. "I need to discuss this with my people before I give you my decision."

Glen nodded. "Fair enough. Discuss. But know that whatever you decide, I leave for Darius at first light, and Roslin's brothers are coming with me. You have until then to decide whether this will be done peacefully." With that, Glen turned and walked away.

Alban was immediately bombarded with questions.

"What are we going to do?" a voice called out.

"We have to give them the boys. We have no choice," another called out. "They'll kill us."

"I can't believe the bunch of you!" Lon shouted bitterly. "Cowards all." He folded his arms over his chest and planted himself in front of the captain of the royal guard. "I forbid you to give in to these renegades. My father is dead. I'm your sovereign now, and I say what happens. Not you." He turned to face the rest of them. "Not any of you."

Alban bowed before him. "What would you have me do, my lord?"

"Fight them."

"What of Lady Roslin? You have no wish to see her?"

"I want to see her," a small voice answered. "I want to go home."

Lon turned to his brother and sneered. "We have no sister. Roslin is one of them now."

"If we fight them, my lord," Alban said, "most of us will be killed, and they'll still take you and your brother. What purpose would that serve?"

"Look at them, Alban. They're not soldiers. They're slaves. Surely, your trained solders can outfight these half-witted animals."

"I would fight them to the death if I thought you and your brother were in danger. I don't believe you are." Alban turned to the others standing around them. "Lon and Kyle are going back to Darius. I believe they'll be safe with Roslin."

Alban signaled to Glen that he had made his decision. "Take them home."

"Coward!" Lon shouted. "You're not fit to wear my father's colors."

Brice sat in his dressing room deep in thought. It had been five days since Roslin had attempted to make love to him. She had respected his wishes and not tried to touch him. Daytime had not been uncomfortable, but when it was time to go to bed, neither knew what to say, so they would cuddle in each other's arms and quietly go to sleep. Brice ached to touch Roslin again, but she had made it clear that night that she too had the same ache inside of her, and he could not bring himself to make love to her again until he knew he would be able to reciprocate. Standing, Brice unwrapped the binding around his chest, letting his breasts fall free. He slipped his nightshirt over his head and walked into the bedchamber to join Roslin.

Roslin opened her eyes and smiled when she heard his footsteps. He climbed into bed and gave her a good night peck, before she turned on her side for sleep. This had become the nightly routine. Roslin would lie on her side, and Brice would hold her. He took a deep breath and snuggled close, wrapping his arms around her middle, pressing his breasts into her back.

Roslin felt the softness of Brice's breasts, instead of the firm unyielding bound chest she was used to. Her heart skipped a beat, as she realized that Brice was finally ready to try to sleep without the bindings. It was a first step. Turning in his arms, she faced Brice. "I love you." She felt Brice tremble as their breasts pressed together, then felt the long body go rigid. "It's all right, love, I just want to hold you, nothing more." She wrapped her arms around him and pressed her lips against his forehead. "Sleep now."

Brice lay in Roslin's arms, needing to talk, but not knowing what to say. A warm wet feeling between his legs interrupted his thoughts. *Damn*, his cycle had started. Another reminder that he was not what he pretended to be. His cycles had always been irregular and could not be predicted. Reluctantly, he extricated himself from Roslin's arms, needing to clean himself.

"Is something wrong?" Roslin asked, as Brice pulled away from her embrace.

"No, nothing's wrong." He slipped out of bed and hurried toward the door. "I'll be right back."

Roslin lay in bed wondering if she had pushed Brice too far again. Had she driven him out of their bed? The more she thought about it, the more she hoped that was not the case. Perhaps it was just a call of nature.

The sound of footsteps drew her gaze to the doorway. Brice stepped into the room and was painted in the soft glow of the full moon streaming through the open window. As he walked toward the bed, Roslin could see his breasts moving under the nightshirt, and the sight took her breath away. It was not that they were extremely large, they weren't, but they were large enough to sway gently as he walked, and Roslin could not take her eyes off them.

When Brice saw where Roslin's eyes were, his arms involuntarily came up to cover his breasts.

"Please don't cover them," Roslin asked. "You have nothing to be embarrassed about. I love looking at you."

Brice let his arms drop to his side and climbed back onto the bed. Roslin scooted over and laid her head on his chest, sliding her hand up his side, stopping just short of his right breast. Brice reached for the hand, and Roslin was sure he was going to remove it, but he picked it up and placed it on top of the breast. Roslin could feel the long body beneath her stiffen and tense up, but Brice did not remove her hand.

"Tell me how you feel," Roslin asked, as she slowly caressed her lover's breast. When he didn't answer, she stilled her hand but kept it where it was. "Please talk to me." She could see beads of sweat appearing on Brice's face, and his breathing was becoming labored.

Brice's jaw clench and his eyes shut tightly. He could feel his heart pounding erratically as the panic grew. "I…I can't…breathe!" he gasped, clutching at Roslin's hand, pushing it away. This was worse than last time. His heart felt like a hammer in his chest, and he thought he was going to suffocate.

Now it was Roslin's turn to panic. "I'll go get help," she said, and started to crawl off the bed.

"No…" Brice gasped out. "Please…don't leave me." Reaching out frantically, he grabbed her arm in a death grip. His distress heightened at the thought of being left alone.

The grip on her arm was crushing, and it hurt, but Roslin made no attempt to remove Brice's hand. Not knowing what else to do, she began caressing Brice's clammy forehead and humming a lullaby that she remembered soothed her when she was young. Ever so slowly, she could see Brice's breathing return to normal. He released her arm, but she didn't move. Tears streamed down her face as she continued humming. It broke her heart that her touch could cause her love such distress. Roslin watched the blue eyes open and focus on her tear-streaked face.

"Please don't cry," Brice said, reaching over to wipe the tears away.

Roslin turned her face into Brice's hand, kissing the palm. "You scared me."

"I scared me, too." Brice took a few much-needed deep breaths. "Nothing like this has ever happened to me before."

"It hurts to know that my touch causes you so much pain." Roslin paused. "Have you ever thought that perhaps something inside you is trying to tell you that you don't really want a woman lover?" New tears started down her face. "They forced you to live as a man all your life, with the fear that you and your loved ones faced possible torture or death if the deception was ever discovered. You couldn't have a man, perhaps your loneliness forced you to seek comfort from women."

"No!" Brice sat up and took Roslin's face in both hands. "No," he spoke softer now. "I love you." He pulled her close. "I'm attracted to you as a woman."

"You're a woman attracted to a woman," Roslin said, trying to understand. "If you can be attracted to a woman, why is it so hard for you to believe I could be?"

Brice looked down at his hands. "I do believe it."

"No, you don't, not really. I don't know how to convince you that it's true. I was attracted to you before I knew the truth about you, but I remember thinking that you weren't like other men. It was that difference that drew me to you." Roslin reached out and lifted Brice's face to make eye contact. "When I saw your breasts, I was both angry and sexually aroused. I was hurt that you lied to me, but finding out you're a woman made the attraction I felt even stronger. I know you find this hard to believe, but it's true. When are you going to get it through your thick head that I'm not like Elsbeth? I love you…" She poked Brice in the chest. "…for who and what you are."

Brice grinned. "Seeing my naked breasts aroused you?"

Roslin blushed and nodded. "Very much."

Brice blushed, too. It was strange but pleasing to think of Roslin admiring his feminine attributes. It was the first time he admitted to himself that perhaps it was not such a tragedy that he was not born a man. *Roslin likes my breasts*. His smile broadened. *Her attraction for me grew stronger because I'm a woman, not in spite of it.* As far as Brice was concerned, he was a man in a woman's body. He had always hated the fact that nature had played such a cruel trick on him. Now it seemed a blessing in disguise. He loved Roslin with all his heart, and she loved him just the way he was. If Roslin was happy he had the body of a woman, he would learn to be happy with it, too. Relief spread through his consciousness at the realization that he no longer regretted the body he was in. If he had a true man's body, Roslin wouldn't want him.

"Does it arouse you to see my naked body?" Roslin asked.

"Oh, yeah," Brice lay back and held out his arms to her. "I love you."

Roslin snuggled into his arms with a sigh. "I love you, too."

Verda Foster

Chapter 12

Roslin worked steadily all morning to prepare a grand supper for the midday meal. One of the scouts Brice had sent out had come back the day before, advising them that Glen should be arriving a little before midday with Roslin's brothers. She wanted everything to be just right and was looking forward to showing off her new cooking skills. Suddenly, strong arms wrapped around her middle, and she was pulled into firm contact with Brice's long, lean body.

He leaned down and kissed her neck. "Something smells good." He gave her a final squeeze, then reached for a loaf of bread that Roslin had just turned out on a rack to cool.

"Ah, ah, ah," Roslin said, smacking his hand away from the loaf. "Not until my brothers get here."

"But I'm hungry." Brice's lips turn down into a pout. "I need something to tide me over."

"Will this do?" Roslin wrapped her arms around his neck and pulled him down for a kiss.

"Mmm," Brice said, forgetting his grumbling stomach. "This will do nicely." He kissed her again, grateful that the awkwardness of touching seemed to have been partially resolved the previous night. He knew he was still not ready to truly surrender, but they were back to being able to kiss and cuddle, and that was wonderful. He was determined that with time he would conquer these unfounded fears.

"Ahem."

Brice and Roslin turned to find Glen standing in the doorway. Roslin rushed to him, throwing her arms around him. "Thank you for bringing my brothers home," she said, looking eagerly over his shoulder but finding no one there. Her eyes tracked back to Glen's, worry showing clearly on her fine features. "You did bring them home, didn't you?"

"I brought them back, but the older boy was not that anxious to come home. They went up to their rooms to change; Lon was complaining about having to wear the same clothes since they left Darius."

Roslin smiled with relief and turned to Brice, patting his belly. "Well, I guess you're going to get to eat before you waste away to nothing." She turned back to Glen and asked, "Would you join us for the midday meal?"

"Thank you, but no. I want to get back to my family."

Roslin kissed him on the cheek. "I want to give Lon and Kyle a week or so to settle in, then invite the whole family over to meet them. I'm hoping Kyle and Bowen will become friends; they're about the same age."

"You just let us know when you want us," Glen said, turning to leave. "We'll be glad to come." With a quick wave, he was gone.

Brice could see the worried expression on Roslin's face, and he hoped with all his heart the reunion with her brothers would go well. After all, she had killed their father and had been agonizing over whether they would accept her explanation that it was an accident. What if they consider her a murderer? Brice pulled her in for a comforting hug. "It'll be all right, you'll see."

Roslin smiled and nodded. "I'll get the food on the table and fetch my brothers; you go call Cadie in from playing and get her cleaned up."

Roslin knocked on the door and held her breath, fearing the reception she might receive. When Kyle opened the door and his face brightened into a smile, she threw her arms around the boy and pulled him in tight. "I've missed you," she said, stepping back to get a better look at him. He looked none the worse for wear. "Are you hungry?" she asked, and received an enthusiastic nod. "Good." Roslin patted his belly. "Because I cooked plenty just in case."

"You don't know how to cook," Lon said sarcastically.

Roslin turned around to find her other brother standing behind her. "Why don't you wait to judge my cooking until you've tasted it?" Roslin said, and Lon rolled his eyes. She opened her arms for a welcoming hug, but Lon turned his back on her. *Give him time, Roslin.* She started walking toward the staircase. "Come on, we better get down there or you'll have to eat it cold."

"Father would have had a slave beaten within an inch of his life if he tried to serve him cold food, but you don't need to worry about that, do you? You killed him."

Roslin stopped and turned around to face her brother. "It was an accident." She looked from one brother to the other, her face pleading for them to believe her. "You saw me. You know that my hands were tied behind by back. The only way I could stop him from killing Brice was to run at him and push him away with my shoulder. I was trying to protect Brice, not kill Father. He stumbled and lost his balance and fell. I only wanted to stop him. Please believe me."

Kyle rushed forward and wrapped his arms around Roslin. "I believe you," he said, glancing nervously at his brother.

Lon sneered at the boy. "You would." He looked back to his sister. "You chose a slave over our father, and he's dead. I'll never forget that. Now that same slave thinks he is sovereign and is using a Ryshtan lady as his bed slave."

"I am not Brice's bed slave!" Roslin said, color rising to her cheeks.

"You deny he has taken you to his bed?"

"I have consented to be Brice's wife and have taken him to my bed for no other reason than that I love him. There are no slaves in Ryshta anymore."

"You committed an act of treason."

Kyle let go of Roslin and turned back to face his brother. "Father hurt Roslin. He was going to kill her."

"He was executing a traitor. That's not the same thing."

"She's not a traitor!"

Roslin stepped between the two boys to prevent the argument from escalating into a physical fight. "Stop this, both of you. Arguing is not going to change what happened." She leaned closer to Lon. "I know in my heart that Father's death was an accident. If you can't accept that, so be it. The subject is closed."

At that moment, Cadie came dancing up the stairs. "Hurry, Mama, we're hungry."

A smile returned to Roslin's face, and she reached out and took the child's hand. "Come then, we wouldn't want you to starve."

"I can't believe you let that little street urchin call you mama," Lon said, looking disgustedly at Cadie.

Roslin felt the flush as anger washed over her, and she was about to lash out at Lon when she felt the little girl clutch her hand tightly. She looked down at Cadie and saw her lip tremble, as tears made their way down her cheeks.

"You still want to be my mama, don't you, ma…Roslin," she said, careful to call her by her name. Now that Roslin's brothers were here for her to take care of, perhaps she would not want a daughter anymore.

Roslin knelt down and pulled the child into her arms. "Of course I do." Leaning away, she cupped her face in her hands. "I love you. You're my little girl now, and nothing is going to change that. Not ever." She wiped the tears from Cadie's face and kissed her forehead before standing to face her brothers. "Brice and Cadie are a part of me now, Lon. We're family. Don't push me to choose you over them because you'll lose."

"You would choose a pretend family…" he nodded at Cadie, "…over your own blood family?"

Roslin's anger flared higher. "She is of our blood. Look at Kyle. Can't you see the family resemblance?" She had not meant to blurt that out and wished immediately that she could take it back.

Lon really looked at Cadie this time. Yes, he could see it. Kyle had been the one who looked like their father, while he and Roslin favored their mother, but this child looked even more like their father than Kyle did. "Why should I be surprised that you've taken in Father's bastard half-breed?"

He turned to Kyle. "You go down and join Roslin's new family if you want to. I choose to eat in my room." He turned and walked down the hallway and into his room, slamming the door behind him.

Cadie looked up at Roslin's flushed face. She had never seen her so angry. She didn't understand Lon's words, but she did understand that they upset Roslin. "Am I a bastard?" Cadie asked. She may not comprehend what it was, but she was sure it was referring to her, and her gaze dropped to the floor, sad to be the cause of Roslin's anger.

"Don't you pay attention to him, little one. He was just trying to make me mad. It has nothing to do with you." Roslin put a finger under the child's chin, lifting her face up so she could look into her eyes. "Okay?"

A smile returned to the girl's face. "Okay."

Roslin knew Brice was going to have a hard enough time with Lon's attitude, without knowing about his verbal attack on her and Cadie. "Let's not tell your papa about this, okay? I need to work out this problem with my brother, and I don't want Brice to worry."

"This is my brother Kyle," Roslin said, as she entered the dining room with the two children. Brice stood and extended his hand to the boy, and he froze.

So this is the new sovereign, he thought, as he took Brice's hand. He was still not sure how he felt about a slave in a position of such power. After all, hadn't his father told him that dimwitted slaves were only suited to menial tasks but nothing that required complicated thought? "I'm pleased to meet you, Lord Brice," he said, bowing his head.

"Just Brice will do," he said, sitting back down. "Welcome to our table." He smiled, trying to reassure the boy. He could see that Kyle was frightened, but that was to be expected. To him, Brice was still the conquering enemy.

Kyle and Cadie sat, and Roslin picked up Lon's plate and began to fill it. "Lon is taking his meal in his room. I'll take this to him and be right back." She looked at the somber faces around the table and started laughing.

"What?" Brice said, starting to laugh himself, as he watched his partner giggle.

"You three look like you just buried your best friend. Now help yourselves to some food, and I'll be back."

Her laughter was contagious, and Kyle and Cadie joined in. The awkward silence broken, everyone filled his or her plates as Roslin left the room.

"Is Cadie really our sister?" Kyle asked, as Roslin tucked him snugly into bed.

"Yes, she really is."

The boy looked thoughtful for a moment. "Do you love her more than me?"

Roslin smiled. "Is that what you've been worrying about?" She received a nod. "I love both of you the same," she said, leaning over to kiss his forehead.

"But you told Lon that if you had to choose, you would pick them over us."

"I love you and Lon. Please don't doubt that. I want you with me. That's why we sent Glen to bring you home. You have a place here with Brice and me for as long as you want it." Roslin ruffled his hair.

"Lon said some very hurtful things and so did I. I hope that we can work out our problem, but if he can't accept Brice and Cadie as family, too, and continues to cause problems, I'm afraid that Brice will ask him to leave. If that happens, I'll stand behind his decision. I can't allow him to tear our family apart. I only pray that he can adapt to our new way of life and we can all go forward as a family." Roslin leaned over and kissed him again. "Sweet dreams," she said, rising and extinguishing the lamp.

What a mess, Roslin thought, as she walked into her dressing room. She hoped Kyle believed that she loved him. Stripping off her clothes, she slipped into her nightgown and joined Brice in their bed. "Kyle was afraid that Cadie was taking his place in my heart."

Brice pulled her close. "Did you make him understand that it wasn't true?"

"I think so," Roslin said, snuggling closer. She was pleased to find that Brice had again removed the bindings before coming to bed. "Thank you for not wearing the bindings. I love the feel of your breasts against my face when I lie on your chest." She pushed herself up to look into impossibly blue eyes. "I was afraid that after your panic last night, you would go back to wearing them again."

"I won't wear them to bed again, I promise." Brice pushed her over onto her back and covered the small body with his own. He leaned down, placing kisses all over Roslin's face, then captured her lips. Rolling over onto his back, he pulled Roslin with him, savoring the feel of her body pressing down on top of him. His breath caught as he felt the familiar panic start, and he pushed it back.

Roslin had felt him momentarily tense, then relax. She smiled. Brice had been able to control the panic this time. She laid her head on Brice's breasts and sighed. This was enough for now. "Good night," she whispered, and closed her eyes, content for the time being with this closeness.

"Good night, love," Brice said, as he kissed the top of her head and thanked whatever higher power sent this precious woman into his life.

Lon woke up and stretched. Even though he hadn't wanted to come home, it felt good to be back in his own bed. This was the first good night's sleep he'd had in what seemed like forever. Even though he had given Roslin a hard time the night before about it, he was glad she was going to marry the new sovereign. At least it allowed Lon to remain in his household, with whatever privilege that entailed. That did not mean, however, that he had to like Brice or approve of his sister's relationship.

A creaking sound brought his gaze to the door, and he saw Kyle peeking through the small opening. "Come on in," Lon said, sitting up and stretching again.

"I was just checking to see if you were awake yet. Roslin sent me up to fetch you for the morning meal." Kyle opened the door all the way and stepped inside.

"Tell her I wish to be served in my room again."

Kyle frowned. He had been worried Lon would say that. He wanted his brother to stop hurting Roslin's feelings, and snubbing the rest of the family was hurtful.

"All right, I'll tell her," the boy said, as he turned to leave.

"Wait." Lon stood and walked over to his little brother. "What is this Brice like?"

"He's…very tall," Kyle answered. "The tallest man I've ever seen. He was nice to me. I…um…I kind of like him."

Lon rolled his eyes. "Oh, please, Kyle, you can't be serious. His influence on Roslin turned her against us and got our father killed."

"She told you that was an accident."

"Yes, a very convenient accident. Brice wanted him dead, and he got Roslin to do it for him."

"You know it wasn't like that," Kyle said, defending his sister. "If you give him a chance, you might like him, too."

"You're pathetic, you know that?" Lon took a step closer to Kyle. "Go back to your pretend family. I don't need Roslin, and I don't need you, either."

Kyle lowered his gaze to the floor and turned to leave, trying not to let Lon see the tears he was holding back.

"Tell Roslin I need a bath before I eat," Lon added, as he watched his brother stride toward the door. "Have her bring water for my bath now; I'm tired of being dirty."

Kyle didn't look back, he just nodded and left the room, closing the door and taking several deep breaths to compose himself before facing Roslin.

Everyone was at the table when Kyle entered the room. Roslin had dished up the porridge already, and a plate of hot biscuits was in the center of the table.

"Where's Lon?" Roslin asked, when she saw the boy enter the dining room alone.

"He said to tell you he wants to eat in his room again." Roslin picked up Lon's porridge and started to rise.

"Lon also said he wants you to fix him a bath before he eats," the boy said, as he sat next to Cadie.

Roslin sighed and started for the kitchen to fetch the buckets for water. Brice reached over and grabbed her arm. He hated seeing the sadness in Roslin's eyes from the way her brother had been treating her. "I'll take care of Lon," he said, pulling out Roslin's chair and beckoning her to sit back down.

"But..."

"I'll take care of it," Brice repeated, his tone gentle, yet firm. "I'm sorry, Roslin, but I won't have Lon treating you as his personal slave. I don't care if he is your brother."

"He just needs time, you'll see."

Brice cupped her face in his hand. "Don't you see that giving in to his demands only reinforces this behavior? He's acting like a spoiled child, and he needs to learn that this is not acceptable."

Roslin knew Brice was right, and she nodded her compliance. She watched Brice's tall frame disappear through the doorway and sighed.

Verda Foster

Chapter 13

Brice walked quickly up the staircase. Lon and Kyle had been home for only a day, and Brice was fast losing his patience. He supposed Lon's arrogance was understandable; after all, he had been groomed to be the next sovereign and was not prepared to become just one of the people. But that was what he was now, and it was time he started pulling his own weight. He opened Lon's door and found the boy lounging on the bed, waiting for his sister to wait on him. Striding into the room, Brice stood at the foot of Lon's bed.

The young man saw the towering figure and knew without a doubt that this was Brice. Refusing to give Brice the respect of a sovereign, he addressed him in a condescending manner, as he would a slave. "Did you fetch the water for my bath?"

"There will be no bath, and if you don't get your sorry behind downstairs now, there will be no meal to break your fast, either."

"First you deny me my birthright and now you won't even let me bathe?"

"You want a bath?" Brice walked to the young man and grabbed him by the arm, pulling him toward the door. "It's time you learned to fix it for yourself."

"I don't do slave work," Lon spat, as Brice dragged him bodily through the door.

"You damn well better learn if you ever plan to bathe again." Brice continued dragging the struggling young man down the stairs and through the large house. Obscenities spewed from Lon's mouth as he tried without success to extricate himself from the ex-slave's grip. Brice stopped at the bottom of the stairs and grabbed Lon's shirt with both hands and shoved him against the wall. Barely contained rage was evident in his eyes. "I will not tolerate such language around my family. Shut your mouth, or I'll shut it for you."

Lon looked into Brice's eyes and for the first time was afraid. He stopped his outburst immediately, his jaw snapping shut.

Brice loosened his grip and let him slide down the wall. "I wanted to try for Roslin's sake to give you a chance to settle in and become accustomed to the new way we do things in your own time. I've changed my mind. You're one of the people now, with no special privileges. It's time you learn that. No one's going to take care of you. You're old enough to take care of yourself." Brice started walking again, pulling Lon along, his long strides making him almost have to run to keep up.

They walked to the tool shed, and Brice grabbed an ax and wedge. "You'll start by cutting the wood to heat the water." He marched Lon to a pile of logs that needed splitting. "You're lucky I don't make you cut down the tree first." Brice picked up a log and hammered the wedge through it with the blunt side of the ax to demonstrate what he wanted the boy to do. "After you split them, you use the other end of the ax to cut them into burning size." He handed Lon the ax and crossed his arms over his chest. "Get to work."

"I hate you!" the boy spat, but quickly took the ax and started to work on the logs.

Brice watched Lon work for an hour, his unused muscles trembling from exertion. When he finally told the boy he could quit, Lon was drenched with sweat, and his hands were blistered and bleeding. "Pick up an armful of wood and follow me," Brice told him, turning and striding toward the house.

Lon followed along, wishing to God he had never asked for a bath.

Brice pointed to the wood box in the corner of the kitchen. "Put the wood in there."

Lon complied and waited silently for his next instructions. Brice showed him how to put wood in the stove and light the fire. "Now go out to the well and bring in water to start heating." He pointed to two metal buckets. "You can only heat two at a time, but it'll take ten buckets of water to fill your tub."

"I can't carry water, my hands are sore." Lon held up his bleeding hands for Brice to inspect.

Brice reached into a drawer and pulled out two towels. "Wrap these around your hands."

"But—"

"Just do it." The tone in his voice brooked no arguments. "Don't fill them too full or you might spill boiling water on yourself when you carry them upstairs."

Lon's eyes grew round. "Why would I heat the water to boiling? I don't want to scald myself."

"How long do you think it takes to heat a bucket of water? By the time the next bucket is hot, the first one would be cold if you didn't heat each one to boiling. Now just do as I say and I'll be back to check on you later."

Lon watched Brice go, his anger somewhat muted by exhaustion. He had been pushing Brice. He knew that, but he hated him for destroying his world, taking away his chance to be sovereign, enticing his sister into killing their father, and betraying the people of Ryshta. Now he realized that his father had been right about Roslin. It disgusted him to watch her voluntarily lowering herself to do menial slave work.

Never in his young life had he been forced to do manual labor. Even though his muscles trembled from overuse, he reluctantly walked to the buckets and picked them up. He hated Brice, but he feared him more. Lon would do as instructed, and his reward would be a nice long soak in a hot bath.

As the days passed, the tension around the house lessened somewhat. Lon seemed to hate everyone and hardly spoke to anyone but Kyle. And poor Kyle…it was so hard for the boy being in the middle like that. He seemed to be adjusting pretty well otherwise. And after seeing what happened to Lon, when Brice said jump, he asked how high.

Glen had sent Bowen over to take him around and show the boy a part of Darius he hadn't even known existed, and the boys were becoming good friends. Kyle did get annoyed sometimes when Cadie tried to tag along, but for the most part, he was coming to terms with having a little sister.

"We need to talk about the wedding," Roslin said, as she snuggled into Brice's shoulder. "Should it be before or after the election?"

"Before, I think," Brice answered, kissing the top of her head. "I don't want to wait. I want to marry you now. It was hard enough to wait for your brothers to come home and get settled in."

Roslin looked up and smiled. "I don't want to wait, either." A thoughtful look crossed her face. She remembered how business-like and formal Ryshtan weddings were. "Do your people always marry someone they love?" she asked, wondering if she and Brice's marriage was only unique to her people.

"Of course," Brice answered. "Why else would someone get married? When you marry, you pledge the rest of your life to that person. I wouldn't want to have to spend my life with someone I didn't love." Brice looked at Roslin questioningly. "Do your people marry without it?"

"Yes, unfortunately, they do. That's why I was at Frama. My father sent me to stay with my grandfather so I could meet the man he had chosen for me."

"He expected you to marry someone you hardly knew?"

Roslin nodded. "I thought I was lucky, really. At least I was given the opportunity to meet my betrothed before the wedding. My mother didn't meet my father until the day of her wedding."

Brice was stunned. "Do all your people marry strangers?"

Roslin became thoughtful again. "I don't know if everyone does, but the upper classes do."

"What would've happened if you didn't like him? How could you let him touch you?"

Roslin remembered the talks she'd had with her mother on this subject. "Well, you just put up with it and do the best you can because it's your duty. Once you marry, you belong to him. When your children come along, you have someone to love, and it makes it all worthwhile. My mother told me that with time, many women learn to love their husbands. She said she hoped that would be the case with me, but if that didn't happen, I would get plenty of love from my children, just as she had from hers."

"What if he doesn't love you and doesn't give you children?"

"Oh, they always give you children. They need an heir to continue their line. Mother said a man doesn't need to love you to have sex with you. She said they stop bothering you once they have enough children to secure their line. Then they keep after their bed slaves and leave you alone to raise their children."

Brice shook his head. "Why would anyone want to live like that?"

"Power, I think. They marry off their children to secure alliances between families of wealth and power. It's good business, nothing more."

Brice shuddered. "I could never do that."

"Now that I know the difference, I couldn't either." Roslin's brow wrinkled. "You know, Brice, I see the way some of your men treat their women, and from the outside, it doesn't look that different from ours."

Brice let his hands wander up and down Roslin's back. He supposed that was true to some extent. "The one major difference is that they begin their life together with love. Then this ego thing gets in the way." Brice thought a moment. "I really think it began for the right reasons. Men believe that women are fragile things that need to be taken care of, which wouldn't be so bad if they didn't carry it to the extreme." Brice continued to let his hands caress the beautiful body in his arms as he spoke, smiling when Roslin sighed and cuddled closer.

"They think women are too sensitive and incapable of taking an equal part in making decisions that affect their future. Her opinion is only considered in matters concerning their children and woman's work. I think it's almost as difficult for our men to see their women as equals, as it is for your people to see mine as more than beasts of burden. In that respect, we all have some adjustments to make."

"You and I are lucky," Roslin said, thinking of all the obstacles they had overcome. "We found each other and fell in love in spite of the differences in the way we were raised and the prejudices we carried for each other's people."

"I count my blessings every day," Brice said, kissing the top of Roslin's head. "The day you become my wife will be the happiest day of my life. Wife, to me, means partner, and I want our wedding to reflect that. When we marry, you won't belong to me. We'll belong to each other."

Roslin smiled. She liked the sound of that. "Yes, we'll belong to each other forever."

They lay in each other's arms for a while, neither speaking, just enjoying the closeness. Roslin turned her face and kissed Brice's breast through his nightshirt. "I love you so much," she said, as she stretched up to kiss his neck.

Brice turned them over and leaned down for a kiss, eagerly exploring Roslin's mouth when Roslin parted her lips. He allowed her to caress his breasts through his nightshirt, and it felt glorious.

As the days passed, they continued to kiss and cuddle and occasionally touch each other's breasts. Each night, Brice felt more and more secure in Roslin's appreciation of the feminine parts of his body.

One evening, they were lying in bed and Roslin was gently massaging his breasts. She thought about how much she loved touching Brice and could not imagine not wanting to touch the person she was in love with. "I don't understand how Elsbeth could say she loved you and not want to touch you."

"She told me she could only respond to my touch if she pictured me as a man. She said to see or touch the real me would spoil everything. She wanted a man. She settled for me." Brice turned on his side and propped his head on his hand. "I loved her, but it was never a complete love. She never truly gave herself, and I lived in fear that she would fall in love with a real man, and she did."

Roslin was stunned. She already knew that Elsbeth pretended Brice was a man, but she hadn't known that she had left him for one. "If she left you, how did you end up with Cadie?"

"He didn't want her. I did. From the moment I knew Elsbeth was with child, I accepted the babe as my own. When Elsbeth was murdered, he was left to raise his own children alone. He didn't want to take on another man's child, too. I loved Cadie before she was born, and I loved her mother. I couldn't leave her in Darius to be branded a slave."

Roslin looked at Brice with a new understanding of why he so desperately concealed his femininity from her. Elsbeth had made him believe he was only worthy of being loved if he hid that part of himself, and even when Brice did as Elsbeth requested, the woman still left him for—as Brice put it—the real thing. No wonder Brice had been terrified to let her see that part of himself. He was afraid it would drive her away, as well.

She found herself hating Elsbeth for doing that to Brice. "I don't understand how you can still love her."

"I hated her for a while, but I couldn't look at my beautiful Cadie and hate her mother."

"Did you know the man she fell in love with?"

Brice nodded. "Yes, I knew him well. He was my brother Dover."

Roslin was stunned. "Oh, Brice, how could they do that to you?"

Brice shrugged. "Dover worked on a farm a few miles away from the city. When he was sent to pick up some seed corn, we hid Elsbeth in the wagon. His wife had died a few months before, and he needed help with his children. Tessa's mother had been caring for them, but her health was failing and Dover needed to take the children home with him. I needed a safe place for Elsbeth, so it seemed like the perfect solution for all of us."

Brice turned on his side. "Looking back, I can see how they would've been drawn to each other. Elsbeth had been so unhappy and lonely, having to stay hidden, and Dover was just getting over losing Tessa."

"What happened?

"Cadie was born about two weeks after Elsbeth moved to the farm, but it was almost three months before I could get permission to go see them. I couldn't wait to see Elsbeth and our new daughter, so I started out well before dawn.

"They were still asleep when I arrived, and I slipped into the room Elsbeth was to share with the children. I wanted to surprise her, but I was the one who got the surprise. She wasn't there.

"Dover's cottage only had two bedchambers, so it wasn't hard to figure out where she was.

"I didn't want to believe it. I tried to come up with a logical reason she wasn't there, but I couldn't."

Brice closed his eyes as the memories washed over him. A tear started down his face, and he felt Roslin's thumb brush it away. His voice was barely audible as he continued.

"I kicked Dover's door open and found them together in his bed. They started awake, and we stared at each other a moment before I ran from the room. I couldn't believe that two people I loved so much would do that to me. When I got outside, my legs wouldn't hold me up and I dropped to the ground and sobbed uncontrollably. Nothing had ever hurt like that.

"Elsbeth came and tried to hold me, but I pushed her away. I yelled at her not to touch me, and she started crying, too. She kept saying, 'I'm sorry,' and 'I didn't mean for you to find out like this.' I managed to get to my feet and started toward my horse. She grabbed my arm, but I pulled it away and turned on her. She shrank back as if she thought I would hit her. That broke my heart even more.

"She told me I was the dearest friend she had ever had and she would always love me. I told her I had seen how much she loved me when I found her in my brother's bed. She said she loved us both, but it was different with Dover. She said it just felt right with him. I thought I knew what she meant by that. She didn't have to pretend that Dover was a man."

Roslin felt her face flush, as anger welled up inside her. "I hate her for doing that to you," she said, wrapping her arms tightly around Brice.

"I don't hate her, and a part of me will always love her. I've thought about it, and I realize that she tried to love me as best she could. I just wasn't right for her, and when she found someone who was…well, I can't blame her anymore. It may sound funny, but when I found myself attracted to you, I felt disloyal to Elsbeth. I thought I could never love anyone as much as I loved her, but I was wrong. I thought what I had with her was true love because I had nothing to compare it with, but what I share with you is so much more. Now I understand what Elsbeth meant when she said 'it just feels right.' Because being with you feels so right for me. I love you."

Chapter 14

Brice put down his napkin, a contented burp slipping out. "That was wonderful," he said, pushing away from the table.

"Thank you," Roslin said. "It's a pleasure to cook for someone who thinks everything I make is wonderful."

Brice leaned over and kissed her, causing Kyle and Cadie to giggle, while Lon sat silently glaring at Brice as usual.

"I need to get back to the stable," Brice said, as he stood and pushed his chair back against the table. "Topka is laboring with her foal, and I want to be there in case she needs help." He looked across the table at Kyle. "Would you like to help?" he asked, and the boy's face lit up.

"Oh, yes, I'll help," Kyle said, jumping to his feet.

"Can I help too, Papa?" Cadie asked sweetly.

"I'm afraid you're too young for this job, little one. You stay here and help your mama." He looked up at Roslin and winked.

"I really could use your help, Cadie," Roslin said, reaching for the little girl's hand and smiling. She was grateful that Brice had been making such an effort to help her brothers. After their initial confrontation, Lon had resisted every effort Brice had made to let him know that he was welcome in their home as long as he followed the rules. Lon had grudgingly taken on the chores assigned to him, and they had had no further clashes, but he never spoke to Brice except to answer a direct question, and his scathing looks made it clear that he detested Brice. Kyle was a different story. He was settling in and making friends and seemed truly happy with his new family.

Brice saw a long gangly back leg emerge from the mare's vagina and frowned. A breach delivery was always difficult and oftentimes deadly.

"You see how we have only one leg coming out?" he asked, speaking calmly so as not to let the boy know he was concerned. Kyle nodded, and Brice continued. "I need to reach inside her and feel around for the other leg to make sure it's not caught on anything."

Kyle frowned. He could not imagine sticking his hands inside the huge animal.

"If she's unable to deliver the foal, they could both die," Brice explained, as he pushed a hand into the opening. Finding the other leg, he gently worked it free and pulled it out to join the other.

Kyle smiled when he saw Brice's hand emerge and pull the other leg out. "Is she going to be all right now?" he asked, finding himself getting excited at the prospect of watching a new life being born.

"With our help, I think she will be." Brice reached back inside with both arms this time. "Grab onto both legs, and when I tell you to pull, I want you to pull with a steady pressure, no big jerks, just steady pressure. Okay?"

Kyle nodded and grabbed the slender legs. "What if I hurt it?" he asked, terrified that he might do something wrong.

"Don't worry, you won't." Brice said, as he felt for the foal's front legs. Finding them, he held them snuggly against the foal's body and waited for the next contraction. "Pull now," he said, as he felt it start. Kyle and Brice both pulled, and the foal slid smoothly along until only its chest, shoulders, and head remained inside.

"You did great," Brice said, smiling at the boy. "One more push should do it." His face sobered momentarily. "Without your help, I might not have been able to get it out in time. Thank you." His eyes turned back to the foal. "It's time," he said, pressing firmly against the foal's ribcage and pulling steadily. The foal emerged, and Brice finished ripping the sack with his strong hands, pulling it away from the colt's head. He grabbed a towel and wiped the foal down, while Kyle looked on in awe. Brice's words played again in his ears. *Without your help, I might not have been able to get it out in time.* He swelled with pride that he had helped save this funny-looking little creature.

The mare nuzzled her newborn and started licking it. "Let's leave them alone to get acquainted," Brice said, handing Kyle a towel to wipe the mess off his hands.

"I can't believe I helped him be born," the boy said, his eyes never leaving the colt.

"Would you like to have him?" Brice asked, placing his hand on Kyle's shoulder. "I think you're old enough for the responsibility, and you did help bring him into the world."

"Yes!" Kyle threw his arms around Brice, then let go just as quickly when he realized what he had done. "I...I'm sorry," he stammered.

"Hey, if you can't hug your family, who can you hug?" Brice pulled the boy back for another embrace.

Kyle's grip tightened around him, as these new words sank in. *Brice considers me part of his family, he's not just being nice because of Roslin.*

"I don't think I've ever seen Kyle so happy," Roslin said, wrapping her arms around Brice. "He's already fallen in love with that colt. He couldn't wait to take Bowen and Cadie over there to show it off."

Brice smiled. "I know. I saw him strutting over there like a proud papa with them in tow."

Lon walked in and stopped in front of Brice. "I'm finished," he said, his face devoid of emotion.

"Good," Brice smiled. "You finished early. Why don't you go on down to the stable? I'm sure Kyle is anxious to show you his colt."

"You may have bought my brother, but you can't buy me," Lon said. "I'm not interested in seeing anything you gave him." He turned and left the room.

Roslin shook her head. "Are we ever going to get through to him?"

"I don't know," Brice said, pulling her close. Lon was such an angry young man, but hopefully, given time, he would come to see they were trying to help him. "I just don't know."

Roslin sat in the large overstuffed chair in her bedchamber and watched Brice pace back and forth. The election was fast approaching, and Mikah had campaigned tirelessly to convince the people that Brice was wrong in letting women vote. He said it was bad enough that Brice had placed two women on the governing council in permanent positions. To let women vote and decide the fate of men was unthinkable. He urged the men not to allow their women to vote. His following was growing, and Brice was surprised to find women falling in with their men in support of Mikah.

He couldn't believe that the women thought so little of their own worth that they would relinquish their voting rights, thinking themselves incapable of making important decisions. Was that the reason? Or were they just not willing to take the risk of angering their men? With three weeks to go until the election, it looked like only a few women were likely to go against their husband's wishes. It was even worse with the single women. They were afraid that if they voted, they would be classified as unsuitable for marriage. After all, what kind of a wife would they make if they considered themselves equal to a man?

"How do they think they can get people to see their point of view if they refuse to express it?" Brice shook his head. "I want all people to have a say, not just the male half of the population."

Roslin got to her feet and blocked Brice's path to halt his pacing. She could see he was getting himself worked up over this and decided to do something about it. "Don't get so upset, love. Change takes time." She took his hand and led him to the chair and pushed him down, then climbed onto his lap. "A few women will vote this election." She leaned over and kissed Brice. "A few more the next." Another kiss. "And before you know it, we'll even have women submitting themselves as candidates." She nuzzled into Brice's neck, nipping and biting, as she worked her way up to a sensitive earlobe.

Brice shivered at Roslin's sensual assault. "You think you have me wrapped around your little finger, don't you?" he asked, trying not to groan as his earlobe was drawn between soft wet lips.

Roslin let go of Brice's ear and sat back with a self-satisfied grin on her face. "Yes, I believe I do."

She let her hands travel to Brice's breasts, caressing them through his nightshirt. Brice's eyes fluttered shut, and this time, he didn't try to stifle the groan. It felt too good.

They had been doing more and more kissing and touching lately but always with their clothes on. Brice no longer panicked when Roslin touched him, and she decided that tonight was the night she was going to try to take the love play further. How far, Roslin was not sure, but she was going to try to get both of them unclothed for a change. Standing, she pulled her nightgown over her head, revealing her nude body. "I want you," Roslin said, extending her hand.

Brice was on his feet in an instant. "It's been too long," he whispered, as he pushed Roslin against the wall. His large hands found Roslin's round firm behind and he lifted her up, extending his thigh so that Roslin was straddling it. "You feel so good," Brice said, thrusting his thigh into her, as he squeezed the firm round globes in his hands. Brice continued to lift Roslin until she could wrap her legs around his waist. Now her breasts were high enough to enjoy Brice's attentions, and he lovingly suckled first one, then the other, all the while using his hands to push Roslin's center into firm contact with his belly.

Roslin arched her back, pushing her breasts harder into Brice's mouth. Each pull on her nipple sent a jolt to her center, and she tightened her legs around her lover, needing the contact.

Brice turned and walked to the bed, placing Roslin down on it, then climbed on top of her. He loved the feel of her beneath him as he thrust against her, making delicious contact. Leaning down, he captured her mouth with his own, exploring its depths with his tongue.

Roslin could feel her release building quickly as Brice's fingers thrust into her moist center. Clutching him tightly, she moaned into his ear.

Brice was floating in the sweet sounds his lover was making, and when he felt Roslin's warm breath against his ear as she moaned his name with her release, he almost joined her with a climax of his own. Roslin stiffened in his arms, then collapsed back down onto the bed, her breathing ragged. Brice lay beside her watching her, his head propped up on his hand.

He remembered the rare times in his youth that he had attempted to pleasure himself and wondered if it would feel different when someone else touched him there. It had felt wonderful to make love to Roslin again, to touch her, and watch her respond. *Nothing could be better than that*, he thought, picking up her hand and pressing it to his lips. He continued watching Roslin, as her breathing returned to normal and her eyes fluttered open, a radiant smile on her face.

"I used to think I knew what love was," Brice said, his hand gently stroking Roslin's belly, then moving up to caress her breast. "But I was so wrong." He leaned down to place a kiss on the breast he was stroking. "I've never felt this deeply about anyone, never felt so…" Brice paused a moment, needing to find the right words. "…complete. My heart is so full of love for you that I feel like it'll burst from the joy of it." His eyes went back to the breast he was caressing. "I love touching you."

Roslin turned on her side to face Brice. "I love to touch you, too," she said, reaching out and cupping her lover's breast through the nightshirt. Then deciding to do something she hadn't tried yet, she leaned over and pulled a nipple into her mouth.

Sensations long denied flooded through Brice, and his body was on fire. He wanted—no, needed—more.

"Wait," Brice said, and Roslin froze. Was she pushing him too fast again?

Brice saw the fear in Roslin's eyes. "I trust your love for me," he said, tracing her lips with his index finger. "I'm not afraid anymore." Brice sat up and pulled his nightshirt over his head. He was wearing no undergarments, and the sight of the lean muscular body took Roslin's breath away.

"Please…I need your touch," Brice said, pulling her close.

Roslin smiled. Those were the words she had been longing to hear, and she threw her arms around him. Brice was so big and strong, power emanated from him, yet at this moment, Roslin had the power, and this knowledge swept through her. She had watched Brice transform into a woman, and she needed to possess this woman… *her woman.* "I love you," she whispered, as she captured Brice's lips in an urgent kiss.

When the kiss ended, Brice allowed Roslin to push him onto his back. He watched her eyes devour his body, desire showing clearly in their green depths.

"Your breasts are beautiful," Roslin said, leaning down to kiss the tip of a hardened nipple. "So beautiful," she repeated, as she began to make love to Brice's breasts.

The fire that had begun to burn spread rapidly through his body until Brice thought he was going to scream, but somehow, he managed to hold it back. The sweet torture Roslin was administering to his breasts was almost more than he could bear. He didn't want to cry out…he couldn't. Women cry out.

Brice clutched Roslin to him tightly, stopping her ministrations and giving himself a moment to catch his breath and think.

When Brice's crushing embrace relaxed a little, Roslin lifted herself up so she could look into his eyes.

"Are you all right?" she said, stroking Brice's sweat-covered forehead.

Brice looked into worried green eyes and melted. "I'm fine...I...it was just going too fast, I thought I was losing control."

"I like knowing I can make you lose control," Roslin said, smiling seductively. "I want you to lose control." She ran her fingers through the coarse dark hair at the apex of Brice's legs, causing him to gasp. "Do you want me to stop?" Roslin asked, taking delight in the way Brice's powerful body quivered beneath her touch.

"No." Brice swallowed the lump in his throat. "Please don't stop." He felt Roslin slowly run her hand up and down the length of his torso, and the smoldering fire burst into full flame again. A groan forced its way from his lips.

"That's good, love, don't hold back, let it out," Roslin said, covering the tall body with her own.

The feel of Roslin's naked body pressed against his own sent Brice soaring. He had not expected to be so overwhelmed by simply pressing their naked bodies together. Roslin slipped off Brice and leaned over, nuzzling into his left breast, causing him to moan loudly, no longer trying to hold back. Both of Brice's hands gripped the bed quilt, as Roslin continued exploring.

Brice gave his body permission to respond—and respond it did. He felt Roslin's small hands stroke the inside of his thighs, and his legs spread wide of their own volition, inviting a more thorough investigation. He could not believe the moans he was hearing were coming from his own mouth and was helpless to stop them. Though in truth, he no longer wanted to stop them. He wanted to experience everything.

Roslin's hands were gentle and tender as they brushed and teased across his center, and Brice thrust his hips upward to make firmer contact.

"Now, I need you inside…now."

Roslin drew a hard nipple into her mouth at the same time she thrust her fingers into Brice.

He released the quilt and gripped her tightly, as if by doing so they could merge into one. "Harder," he pleaded, thrusting his hips to set a rhythm for Roslin to follow. Brice screamed out as his first orgasm crashed through his body, and he clutched Roslin so tightly that she could hardly breathe. When it was over and Brice could breathe again, he raised his hands to wipe the tears that were flowing from his eyes. They were tears of joy, and he smiled at how wonderful it felt to finally allow himself to accept the pleasure that Roslin so wanted to share with him. He pulled Roslin up for one more kiss. "Thank you for not giving up on me."

Chapter 15

Brice stood in the meeting hall and looked out over the crowd of gathered women. He had sent word that there would be a meeting of women only and made it clear that attendance was compulsory. This way, they would not have to argue with their men to attend.

"I'm not advocating a war between the genders, that's not what this meeting is about," Brice said to the room full of women. "But I'm going to assure that all people, regardless of their gender, be allowed to have a say in how they're governed." Brice paused, his eyes sweeping the room. The women seemed torn between taking a step closer to equality with men and not making waves and letting their men have their way.

"You can't understand what it's like to be a woman," someone sitting to the side called out. "You have nothing to lose, you're a man." Several of the women nodded their agreement. "Walk a mile in our shoes and see if you feel the same."

Brice realized they were right. He may have been born female, but no one knew it. The respect and leadership that had been given him was based on the fact that everyone believed him to be a man. They never would have followed him if they had known the truth. Perhaps it was time to end the lie. Maybe if they knew what he really was, they would see that a woman could lead as well as any man.

"You're right," Brice said, walking over to Roslin and taking her hand for moral support. "I don't really know what it's like to be a woman." He squeezed the small hand. "But there is a truth about me that I want to share with you." He looked at Roslin, and she smiled at him and gave a small nod of approval. Brice's heart pounded and his mouth went dry. The panic began to engulf him, and he let the calming influence of Roslin's presence push it away. There was no going back. He gripped Roslin's hand harder and thanked God she was here with him. "I was born a girl, but my parents chose to raise me as a male to protect me from the Ryshtans."

There was a collective gasp in the room, then complete silence, as the women tried to digest this unbelievable information.

"I could have continued to lie to you, but I wanted you to see that the only limitation you have is what you allow others to put on you." Brice turned to Roslin and smiled. "I won't do that anymore. I want to be who I am, no matter the consequences. I want that for all of us. Change is a difficult thing, but that doesn't make it undesirable." Brice felt the panic dissipate as the weight of the lie he had been living with was lifted off his shoulders. It felt surprisingly good to be free of it.

"Please don't limit yourselves. Your men should be your partners, not your taskmasters. If you truly do not want to express your opinion with your vote, that's your choice. I respect that. But don't allow someone else to make the decision for you. It's your right as a free person. Don't throw it away." Brice turned and escorted Roslin from the room, leaving the women of Darius to ponder his words.

"We need to call the children together and tell them before someone else does," Roslin said, as they returned from the meeting.

"I know we should've told them first, but I hadn't planned to tell anyone when I started talking." Brice looked at Roslin and smiled. "It just happened." Brice knew Roslin was responsible for helping him come to terms with who he really was and being able to say it out loud in a room full of people. It felt good to be free of hiding what he was from people he cared about. "Kyle and Cadie will be at the stable with the colt," Brice said, stopping and looking in that direction. "I'll go fetch them and you go in and see if Lon is home."

Roslin nodded and continued up the palace steps.

Cadie and Kyle smiled and chatted with each other, while Lon sat quietly watching them. He couldn't understand why Kyle was nice to the brat. They all sat in comfortable chairs in the large sitting room that was just off the great hall. They couldn't help but wonder what was so important they had to drop what they were doing and meet together like this.

Brice and Roslin appeared in the doorway, and the room became quiet, as all eyes turned in their direction. "I have something I need to tell you," Brice said, stepping into the room. Roslin followed him in and sat next to Kyle. "What I have to say is not going to change anything in our family, but it's something you need to know." Brice let his eyes rest on each of them momentarily, then he continued. "When I was a small child, just a little younger than Cadie, my parents decided to raise me as a male child, even though I was born a girl."

Kyle's eyes grew round with surprise, while Lon just rolled his eyes and shook his head.

"If you were born a girl, how did you turn into a boy?" Cadie asked, confusion showing plainly on her face.

"I didn't," Brice said, kneeling in front of his daughter. "Technically, I'm still a girl."

Cadie frowned. "Are you still my papa?"

Brice scooped the girl up in his arms. "I'll always be your papa. That won't change."

"Okay," Cadie said, a smile returning to her face.

Brice looked at Kyle and Lon, who had remained silent. "Nothing is going to change around here. I'm not going to start wearing petticoats and looking for the man of my dreams." He looked at Roslin, who had let a laugh slip out at the picture Brice had just painted. "I already found the woman of my dreams." He took Roslin's hand and pulled her to her feet. "Roslin is going to be my wife, and we're all a family. That hasn't changed." Brice wrapped his arms around Roslin, pulling her close. "What will change is that everyone else will know the truth about me, and they might give you a hard time because of it. I hope that doesn't happen, but we wanted to tell you ourselves before someone else did."

Kyle stood up. "I'll punch anyone who says anything bad about you."

Brice smiled. "Thank you, Kyle, but I don't want you getting into fights defending me. I can take whatever they say about me, as long as I know my family is okay with it."

"I'm okay with it," Kyle said. "But what kind of a man would I be if I didn't defend my family? I'm sorry, but I think I'll have to punch 'em if they say anything bad."

Lon stood up. "If that's all, can I leave now?"

Roslin nodded and he walked away.

"Well, what did he want?" Mikah asked, as his daughter Sharlyn walked through the door. He had been surprised when Brice had called a women-only meeting and was glad he had a daughter he could send who would report back to him.

She looked at her father, wondering what his reaction would be when she told him that The Chosen was a woman. "Brice told us we shouldn't let our men folk intimidate us. That we should have faith in our opinions and not be afraid to express them."

Mikah shook his head, wondering how the man could possibly believe women should be taken seriously. "Is that all?" he asked, wondering why they needed a meeting for something so unimportant.

"No, that's not all," Sharlyn answered. "Brice also explained that given a chance, a woman can be just as effective a leader as a man can, and to prove it…" She held her breath a moment before blurting the news out. "…She told us that she's a woman."

Mikah's jaw dropped open, and he shook his head in disbelief. It couldn't be true. He had known Brice basically all his life. "You're sure you heard him correctly?" he asked, looking skeptically at his eldest child.

"I'm sure I heard *her* correctly," Sharlyn responded. "She said she's living proof that a woman is capable of doing more than traditional woman's work."

"I don't believe it. This is just a trick to make women think they should be considered equal to men." Mikah turned and started to pace. "It won't work, though. No one's going to believe such a ridiculous story."

"If you had heard her, you'd believe it," Sharlyn said. "I believed her, and the other women there believed her, too."

Mikah stopped short, a smile slowly spreading across his face. This might work to his advantage after all. If it was true, it was not only evidence that Brice was just an inferior woman, but it also proved him to be a liar. If it proved false, it still showed him to be a liar. Either way, Mikah won. He was certain he could convince the people not to follow someone they could not trust.

Once their faith in Brice was shaken, he could get them to throw out this ridiculous permanent council and simply elect a leader and let him choose his own advisers. This would give him a good chance of taking over the power in Ryshta.

Word spread rapidly, and soon all of Darius knew their leader was physically a woman. When Brice heard the bell sounding to call the people for an impromptu meeting, he was certain he knew what the topic of discussion would be. He vacillated about whether to go or let everyone get used to the idea before facing them, finally deciding it was better to face their questions now, rather than wait and wonder what was going on.

When he arrived at the meeting ground, he found the people were not angry but confused. In that state, they were easily manipulated by Mikah, who was doing his best to sway them to his way of thinking. He made it clear that he thought they should toss Brice out on his ear and choose a new leader.

"…and how can we continue to put our faith in a leader who has been lying to us all her life?" Mikah pointed at Brice, as the crowd parted to let him through.

"You don't understand," Shea said, raising her voice to draw the attention away from Mikah. "Brice had no choice in the matter. He was only a babe when his father and I decided to raise him as a male."

All eyes turned to the older woman, wanting to hear what she had to say. "Once Brice was counted as a boy, we had no choice but to continue, for to do anything else would have meant severe punishment or possible death for our family."

"What about these last five years? There were no Ryshtans standing over her shoulder, ready to dole out punishment," Mikah said, turning once again to the crowd. "I can understand why she kept up the pretense while she was here, but for the last five years, she has been free of them. She could have given up this charade and lived as a decent woman. Instead she continued the deception even though it was no longer necessary to keep her family safe. No, she preferred to lie to the people who trusted her, taking on a woman lover to perpetuate this deviant lifestyle. This was a choice." He looked at Brice and asked point blank, "Why did you continue to live as a man when you left Darius?"

"I lived the way I've always lived, the way that's comfortable for me. People assumed I was a man, and I did nothing to change their perception of me. If you want to call that lying, then yes, I lied. There was more than one reason I let people believe I was a man," Brice continued. "First, I didn't want to shake the confidence my soldiers had in me as their leader. If we were going to win our freedom, we had to pull together, gathering momentum as we liberated Ryshta, city by city. The slaves we encountered in each new city didn't know me and might have been reluctant to join us if they knew I was a woman. What we were doing was too important to take that risk. Second, but just as important to me is…" He looked Mikah in the eye. "…I did not then, nor do I now, plan to change the way I live. I don't care if you call me he or she. It makes no difference to me because what you label me doesn't define who I am. What you see right now is how I'm most comfortable. I'm in love with a woman, and I won't give her up to please anyone." He thumped his chest with his fist. "This is not a lie, it's the real me." Brice looked from face to face and repeated, "This *is* who I am. I haven't changed at all except for what you choose to call me. I'm the same person I was before you found out the truth of my gender. Can't you understand that nothing about me has changed?"

"Everything has changed," Mikah said, glaring at Brice. He turned back to the crowd. "Can't you see what she's trying to do?" He purposefully let his eyes skip from man to man, never making eye contact with the women in the group. "She's putting ideas into our women's minds, and they're starting to question our decisions." He glared at Brice momentarily, then his gaze returned to the gathering. "She's planning on marrying another woman. Where does that leave us if our women start pairing up with each other?"

"I'm not advocating that women pair up with each other to the exclusion of men," Brice said, exasperation clear in his voice. "What I said was that I'm in love with a woman and I don't intend to give her up. I believe that people should follow their hearts.

Love is a beautiful gift and should never be thrown away because you fall in love with someone who perhaps others might not approve of." He looked at Roslin and smiled. "I hope you people can accept my love for Roslin, but if you don't, that won't change my feelings for her or stop me from pledging the rest of my life to her. People don't all have to be the same. Be who you are, and together we'll go forward as a free people who respect one another's diversity."

A large ruddy-faced man stepped out of the throng and turned to face them. "I don't give a damn what Brice is or who he chooses to love. He has been a good friend and a good leader. Without him, we would still be slaves. He gave us the courage to win our freedom. Would anyone here prefer to go back to the way things were?"

The few Ryshtans in the group were quiet, but everyone else vehemently called out, "No! Brice is The Chosen, sent to lead us—"

"That's another lie," Mikah said, interrupting. "Brice couldn't be The Chosen. The prophecy said The Chosen was a man."

Egan, the old priest, stepped forward. "No, you're wrong," he said, looking Mikah in the eye. "I've read the passage many times. There's no mention of gender, only that The Chosen would step from the masses to lead our people out of slavery and into a new life. The only description given was that The Chosen was tall as the trees, with eyes the color of the sacred crystal." He turned to face the crowd. "I don't know about the rest of you, but I for one believe Brice is The Chosen. He fits the description, and he fulfilled the first part of the prophecy—he led us out of slavery. Now Mikah is trying to stop him from completing the prophecy." The old man looked at Brice and smiled. "Brice *is* The Chosen, and I'll follow where he leads."

The priest spoke eloquently, and although the issue of Brice's gender had momentarily confused the people, the facts spoke for themselves. If the great Earth spirits chose Brice, who were they to question the ancient wisdom? The crowd erupted with support for him. Circling Brice and cheering, they lifted him onto their shoulders and walked away en masse, chanting his name, leaving a bewildered Mikah behind.

Roslin stood and watched as the crowd carried Brice away. She swallowed the lump in her throat and sighed. It was finally over. They saw Mikah for what he was and accepted Brice as he was. There would be no more opposition to the governing council or the right of women to vote.

"I should've known he would win," Lon said, walking to where his sister stood in front of the dais. "Those people really are as stupid as Father said they were." He had hoped the people would rebel again and throw Brice out. It had certainly not proven to be an advantage living under his roof, as he had first thought. Now he just wanted him gone, but that was not going to happen. He knew that now. It was time for him to leave the nest, and now seemed as good a time as any to join one of the emigrating groups of Ryshtans leaving Darius.

"I wish you could understand that we all won," Roslin said, trying not to let her brother's words spoil the warm feeling that seeing the people embrace Brice had caused.

"I've decided that I can't live under your roof any longer," Lon said, ignoring his sister's words. "It was bad enough being ordered around by a man, but it's intolerable from a woman. I've spoken to my friend Adler's father about joining them when they leave in the morning for Frama." He looked at Roslin, and she could see determination in his eyes. "I don't belong here anymore."

Roslin let him finish speaking and sighed. She had so hoped that he would open his stubborn eyes and really see what they were trying to do here. "If that's what you want to do, we won't try to stop you." She walked closer and put her hand on his shoulder. "If you ever want to come home and be a part of our family, you'll be welcome."

Lon shrugged her hand off. "I have no family." He turned and walked away.

Roslin wasn't surprised that he wanted to go. Ever since the rebels took control of Darius, the Ryshtans had been leaving in small groups to make a home elsewhere. Some chose to stay, refusing to be driven out of their homes, but more and more were leaving every day, wanting to go where they were not so greatly outnumbered by people who despised them. They understood that wherever they went in Ryshta, the new rules applied.

Kyle stood and watched his brother pack his belongings. "I don't want you to go," he said, his eyes pleading with Lon to reconsider leaving.

Lon looked at the boy and shook his head. "I have to go. You know how Brice treats me." His jaw clenched. "I hate him."

"Will I ever see you again?" Kyle asked, his voice cracking.

"I'm never coming back." Lon picked up another bag and started to stuff it. "If you want to see me, you'll have to come to Frama. I'm going to go claim Grandfather Gage's house as his eldest heir."

"Roslin's older than you are."

"You know women don't count in things like this."

"They do now."

"Well, I doubt she's going to leave Brice and go claim it." He finished packing the last bag and looked around the room to see if he was forgetting anything important. "You could come with me if you want," Lon said, looking back at his brother. "I don't think Roslin will force you to stay if you really want to go."

Kyle shook his head. He loved his brother, but he didn't want to leave Roslin and the new family he had become a part of. Roslin had made it clear to him how much she loved and wanted him with her. Brice had gone out of his way to make him feel special and welcome and a part of his family. He even had to admit that his pest of a little sister was starting to grow on him, too. For the first time in his life, he felt part of a family that truly cared for one another.

"Suit yourself," Lon said, as he shouldered one bag and picked up two more. "Get that one for me," he said, nodding to the last bag.

Kyle picked up the bag and sadly followed his brother out the door.

Egan, the high priest, watched as Roslin and Brice walked into the small chapel, hand in hand. "To what do I owe this pleasure?" he asked, as they drew near.

"As you know, I've asked Roslin to marry me, and she has consented." Brice looked down at Roslin and flashed a radiant smile that was returned in kind.

Egan nodded and smiled at the young couple.

"I know that I was not raised in your faith," Roslin said, holding tightly to Brice's hand. "But Brice and I want to start our life together with the traditional ceremony of his people. We would be honored if you would preside."

The old priest took Roslin's hand. "You and Brice worked together to free my people, and I would be honored to join you in marriage." Egan looked from Roslin to Brice. "You'll each have tasks to perform in preparation for the joining." He placed his hand on Brice's shoulder. "You will prepare the circle." Brice nodded, and the old priest dropped his hand back to his side and continued. "The circle will be built with cedar logs, and you will tend the fire for three days to purify the circle. The first morning, the two of you will ask the blessing of the spirit of the earth and all growing things. The second morning, you will ask the blessing of the spirit of the wind. The last morning, you will seek the final blessing from the spirit of the fire." He looked back to Brice. "After the final blessing, you will let the fire burn down to coals for the ceremony. During the three days of blessing and purification, you will also compose the words that signify this joining in your hearts. Write the words together, and your hearts will speak as one."

Brice prepared the circle of logs as he had been instructed and tended it faithfully for three days. Each morning, they joined hands and knelt in front of the circle and requested the blessing. Each evening, they looked into their hearts to find the words that would define their union.

It was time. The cedar logs had been burned to glowing embers, and Brice and Roslin waited together for the wedding party to approach the circle, led by Egan. Immediate family and friends would be allowed into the small circle, while the rest of the people who had gathered to celebrate the union of The Chosen and his lady stood back and watched as the wedding party approached the circle of embers.

"We gather on this day to celebrate the love of Brice and Roslin and to sanctify their union. Let us begin therefore by leaping the fire, which is an ancient act of purification." The priest jumped into the circle, then stepped aside, allowing Brice and Roslin to jump over the embers, followed by the rest of the wedding party. The guests linked hands to form a circle around Brice, Roslin, and the priest.

Egan walked to the glowing embers and bent down, lighting a candle. "As you hold the sacred flame, receive its blessing of passion and energy. This relationship you are entering into is strong because it shines with love and mutual devotion, concern for the happiness of the other, and joy in each other's company. There is nothing stronger than this bond of love." The old priest handed the candle to Brice and Roslin, who each reached out with one hand.

Egan turned and retrieved a chalice from the wedding table and held it out in front of Brice and Roslin. "This joining is only affirming what already exists in the silent places of your hearts. It is yours to define, yours to make real, and yours to live. Are there symbols of this union that you wish to exchange?"

Brice took a shaky breath and reached into his pocket, pulling out a ring. Bringing it to his lips, he kissed it reverently and placed it in the chalice. He thought his heart would burst with joy, as he watched the woman he loved place a ring in the chalice, as well.

"May these rings be blessed and may they ever be a reminder of the love shared here today." The priest held the chalice up for all to see, then brought it back down in front of the couple. "It's time to speak what's in your hearts."

Brice and Roslin faced each other and clasped hands.

Brice was not sure he could speak, he was so overcome with emotion. He looked into Roslin's beautiful green eyes, and the words they had written together started to spill from his lips with no effort.

"I, Brice, in the name of the spirits that reside within us all and the love that fills my heart to bursting, take you, Roslin, to be my chosen one. To desire you and be desired by you, without sin or shame, for sin and shame cannot exist within the purity of my love for you. I promise to love you in this life and beyond, where we shall meet, remember, and love again. I shall not seek to change you. I shall respect you, your beliefs, your people, and your ways as I respect myself." Brice reached a trembling hand into the chalice and retrieved the small silver band, slipping it reverently on Roslin's finger, then lifting her hand and kissing it, as a single tear made its way down his face.

Roslin reached up and wiped away the tear. "I, Roslin, in the name of the spirits that reside within us all and by the love that fills my heart, take you, Brice, to be my chosen one. To desire and be desired by you, without sin or shame, for sin and shame cannot exist within the purity of my love for you. I promise to love you in this life and beyond, where we shall meet, remember, and love again. I shall not seek to change you. I shall respect you, your beliefs, your people, and your ways as I respect myself." Now it was Roslin's turn to slip a ring on Brice's finger. His hand was trembling so that it took a moment for Roslin to get the ring on. She smiled at Brice, then they turned together to face the priest again.

"May your love so endure that its flame remains a guiding light unto you." Egan smiled at them. "It's traditional for the couple to jump the broom. This represents the transition into a new life. Will one member of each of your families step forward?" Glen and Kyle stepped out of the circle and held the broom low to the ground, while Brice and Roslin jumped across it.

"Go now together. Greet your brothers and sisters and receive their blessings."

Brice and Roslin walked around the circle hand in hand, receiving congratulations from friends and family.

Egan and his assistant retrieved cakes and ale from the small table behind them and followed behind the couple, passing them out.

"Eat and drink. Share and be happy."

When Roslin and Brice completed the circle, they each took one cake and one glass of ale. "And as we share, let us remember that all we have we share with those who have nothing. So shall it be." Brice offered Roslin a bite, then a sip of ale, and received the same in return.

Brice took both of Roslin's hands in his own and brought them to his lips, kissing each palm in turn. They had pledged themselves to each other many times before, but somehow this was different...it was more. Perhaps it was because they had evoked the blessings of the spirits. He felt a connection to Roslin that he knew nothing in this world or any other could sever.

Leaning down, he kissed Roslin's upturned lips, then pulled her close, burying his face in golden tresses. "I love you," he whispered, as he felt Roslin's arms tighten around him. "I wouldn't change anything in my past because it led me to this moment and to you."

Roslin was overcome by the sentiments. Tears began to fall, and she couldn't speak. She just nodded and pressed her wet face into Brice's neck. An involuntary shudder went through her body at the thought that this joy almost wasn't hers. Of the life she would have led if things had been different and she had married Amon.

Releasing Roslin, Brice cupped her wet face in his hands, wiping the tears away with his thumbs. Clasping hands, they stepped across the fading embers and walked together toward their new life.

Verda Foster

ABOUT THE AUTHOR

Verda Foster has worked in and around the arts and craft industry for twenty years, and you can often find her judging at one of the many ceramic and craft shows held throughout Southern California.

She has been teaching the art of painting statuary for thirteen or fourteen years and enjoys seeing students' eyes light up when they see a piece of white-ware come to life in their hands.

Other novels by Verda Foster

These Dreams
Haunted from childhood by visions of a mysterious woman she calls Blue Eyes, artist Samantha McBride is thrilled when a friend informs her that she has seen a woman who bears the beautiful face she has immortalized on canvas and dreamed about for so long. Thrilled by the possibility that Blue Eyes might be a flesh and blood person, Samantha sets out to find her, certain the woman must be her destiny.

When Tess Richmond becomes aware that a P.I. has been hired to investigate her, she plans to teach the woman a lesson she won't soon forget, never suspecting the terrible mistake she's about to make and the fragile heart she'll decimate in the process.

Samantha's first meeting with Tess ends in an act of heartbreaking cruelty that leaves her shattered. When Tess realizes her mistake, she wants to make amends, but can she rebuild the trust that was lost or the love that was denied?

The Gift
Detective Rachel Todd doesn't believe in Lindsay Ryan's visions of danger, even when the horrifying events Lindsay predicted begin to come true. That mistake could cost more than one life before this rollercoaster ride is over.

Graceful Waters, co-authored with BL Miller
Joanna Carey, senior instructor at Sapling Hill, wasn't looking for anything more than completing one more year at the facility and getting closer to her private dream—a small cabin on a quiet lake. She was tough and smart and had a plan for her life.

When Carey meets angry and disillusioned Grace Waters, neither is prepared for what comes next. Grace meets her match in Carey, the strong and disciplined woman who's determined to help Grace help herself. Together they will change each other's lives in ways that neither thought possible.

Crystal's Heart, co-authored with BL Miller
Crystal Sheridan is a professional stripper, straight, alcoholic, and drug user. Laura Taylor is a professional writer, lesbian, obsessive tidier, and control freak. Two women who have nothing in common are amazed to find they can live together when they become improbable housemates. As Laura helps Crystal come to terms with her traumatic past, romance blossoms. The writer finds healing for her own wounds as Crystal recovers her life and shows Laura another side to love.

Other Intaglio Publications Titles

Accidental Love, by B. L. Miller, ISBN: 1-933113-11-1, Price: 18.15
What happens when love is based on deception? Can it survive discovering the truth?

Code Blue, by KatLyn, ISBN: 1-933113-09-X, Price: $16.95 - Thrown headlong into one of the most puzzling murder investigations in the Burgh's history, Logan McGregor finds that politics, corruption, money and greed aren't the only barriers she must break through in order to find the truth.

Counterfeit World, by Judith K. Parker, ISBN: 1-933113-32-4, Price: $15.25
The U.S. government has been privatized, religion has only recently been decriminalized, the World Government keeps the peace on Earth—when it chooses—and multi-world corporations vie for control of planets, moons, asteroids, and orbits for their space stations.

Crystal's Heart, by B. L. Miller & Verda Foster, ISBN: 1-933113-24-3, Price: $18.50 - Two women who have absolutely nothing in common, and yet when they become improbable housemates, are amazed to find they can actually live with each other. And not only live...

Gloria's Inn, by Robin Alexander, ISBN: 1-933113-01-4, Price: $14.95 - Hayden Tate suddenly found herself in a world unlike any other, when she inherited half of an inn nestled away on Cat Island in the Bahamas.

Graceful Waters, by B. L. Miller & Verda Foster, ISBN: 1-933113-08-1, Price: $17.25 - Joanna Carey, senior instructor at Sapling Hill wasn't looking for anything more than completing one more year at the facility and getting that much closer to her private dream, a small cabin on a quiet lake. She was tough, smart and she had a plan for her life.

I Already Know The Silence Of The Storms, by N. M. Hill, ISBN: 1-933113-07-3, Price: $15.25 - I Already Know the Silence of the Storms is a map of a questor's journey as she traverses the tempestuous landscapes of heart, mind, body, and soul. Tossed onto paths of origins and destinations unbeknownst to her, she is enjoined by the ancients to cross chartless regions beset with want and need and desire to find the truth within.

Incommunicado, by N. M. Hill & J. P. Mercer, ISBN: 1-933113-10-3, Price: $15.25 - Incommunicado is a world of lies, deceit, and death along the U.S/Mexico border. Set within the panoramic beauty of the unforgiving Sonoran Desert, it is the story of two strong, independent women: Cara Vittore Cipriano, a lawyer who was born to rule the prestigious Cipriano Vineyards; and Jaquelyn "Jake" Biscayne, an FBI forensic pathologist who has made her work her life.

Infinite Pleasures, Stacia Seaman & Nann Dunne (Eds.), ISBN: 1-933113-00-6, Price: $18.99 - Hot, edgy, beyond-the-envelope erotica from over thirty of the best lesbian authors writing today. This no-holds barred, tell it like you wish it could be collection is guaranteed to rocket your senses into overload and ratchet your body up to high-burn.

Josie & Rebecca: The Western Chronicles, by Vada Foster & BL Miller, ISBN: 1-933113-38-3, Price: $18.99 - At the center of this story are two women; one a deadly gunslinger bitter from the injustices of her past, the other a gentle dreamer trying to escape the horrors of the present. Their destinies come together one fateful afternoon when the feared outlaw makes the choice to rescue a young woman in trouble. For her part, Josie Hunter considers the brief encounter at an end once the girl is safe, but Rebecca Cameron has other ideas....

Misplaced People, by C. G. Devize, ISBN: 1-933113-30-8, Price: $17.99 - On duty at a London hospital, American loner Striker West is drawn to an unknown woman, who, after being savagely attacked, is on the verge of death. Moved by a compassion she cannot explain, Striker spends her off time at the bedside of the comatose patient, reading and willing her to recover. Still trying to conquer her own demons which have taken her so far from home, Striker is drawn deeper into the web of intrigue that surrounds this woman.

Murky Waters, by Robin Alexander, ISBN: 1-933113-33-2, Price: $15.25 - Claire Murray thought she was leaving her problems behind when she accepted a new position within Suarez Travel and relocated to Baton Rouge. Her excitement quickly diminishes when her mysterious stalker makes it known that there is no place Claire can hide. She is instantly attracted to the enigmatic Tristan Delacroix, who becomes more of a mystery to her every time they meet. Claire is thrust into a world of fear, confusion, and passion that will ultimately shake the foundations of all she once believed.

Picking Up The Pace, by Kimberly LaFontaine, ISBN: 1-933113-41-3, Price: 15.50 - Who would have thought a 25-year-old budding journalist could stumble across a story worth dying for in quiet Fort Worth, Texas? Angie Mitchell certainly doesn't and neither do her bosses. While following an investigative lead for the Tribune, she heads into the seediest part of the city to discover why homeless people are showing up dead with no suspects for the police to chase.

Southern Hearts, by Katie P Moore, ISBN: 1-933113-28-6, Price: $16.95 - For the first time since her father's passing three years prior, Kari Bossier returns to the south, to her family's stately home on the emerald banks of the bayou Teche, and to a mother she yearns to understand.

Storm Surge, by KatLyn, ISBN: 1-933113-06-5, Price: $16.95 - FBI Special Agent Alex Montgomery would have given her life in the line of duty, but she lost something far more precious when she became the target of ruthless drug traffickers. Recalled to Jacksonville to aid the local authorities in infiltrating the same deadly drug ring, she has a secret agenda--revenge. Despite her unexpected involvement with Conner Harris, a tough, streetwise detective who has dedicated her life to her job at the cost of her own personal happiness, Alex vows to let nothing--and no one--stand in the way of exacting vengeance on those who took from her everything that mattered.

These Dreams, by Verda Foster, ISBN: 1-933113-12-X, Price: $15.75 - Haunted from childhood by visions of a mysterious woman she calls, Blue Eyes, artist Samantha McBride is thrilled when a friend informs her that she's seen a woman who bears the beautiful face she has immortalized on canvas and dreamed about for so long. Thrilled by the possibility that Blue Eyes might be a flesh and blood person, Samantha sets out to find her, certain the woman must be her destiny.

The Cost Of Commitment, by Lynn Ames, ISBN: 1-933113-02-2, Price: $16.95
Kate and Jay want nothing more than to focus on their love. But as Kate settles in to a new profession, she and Jay become caught up in the middle of a deadly scheme—pawns in a larger game in which the stakes are nothing less than control of the country.

The Last Train Home, by Blayne Cooper, ISBN: 1-933113-26-X, Price: $17.75
One cold winter's night in Manhattan's Lower East side, tragedy strikes the Chisholm family. Thrown together by fate and disaster, Virginia "Ginny" Chisholm meets Lindsay Killian, a street-smart drifter who spends her days picking pockets and riding the rails. Together, the young women embark on a desperate journey that spans from the slums of New York City to the Western Frontier, as Ginny tries to reunite her family, regardless of the cost.

The Price of Fame, by Lynn Ames, ISBN: 1-933113-04-9, Price: $16.75 - When local television news anchor Katherine Kyle is thrust into the national spotlight, it sets in motion a chain of events that will change her life forever. Jamison "Jay" Parker is an intensely career-driven Time magazine reporter; she has experienced love once, from afar, and given up on finding it again...That is, until circumstance and an assignment bring her into contact with her past.

The Gift, by Verda Foster, ISBN: 1-933113-03-0, Price: $15.35 - Detective Rachel Todd doesn't believe in Lindsay Ryan's visions of danger, even when the horrifying events Lindsay predicted come true. That mistake could cost more than one life before this rollercoaster ride is over. Verda Foster's The Gift is just that – a well-paced, passionate saga of suspense, romance, and the amazing bounty of family, friends, and second chances. From the first breathless page to the last, a winner.

The Value of Valor, by Lynn Ames, ISBN: 1-933113-04-9, Price: $16.75
Katherine Kyle is the press secretary to the president of the United States. Her lover, Jamison Parker, is a respected writer for Time magazine. Separated by unthinkable tragedy, the two must struggle to survive against impossible odds...

With Every Breath, by Alex Alexander, ISBN: 1-933113-39-1, Price: $15.25
Abigail Dunnigan wakes to a phone call telling her of the brutal murder of her former lover and dear friend. A return to her hometown for the funeral soon becomes a run for her life, not only from the murderer but also from the truth about her own well-concealed act of killing to survive during a war. As the story unfolds, Abby confesses her experiences in Desert Storm and becomes haunted with the past as the bizarre connection between then and now reveals itself. While the FBI works to protect her and apprehend the murderer, the murderer works to push Abby over the mental edge with their secret correspondence.

Intaglio Publication's Forthcoming Releases

Coming in 2005

November
Halls of Temptation, by Katie Moore, ISBN: 1-933113-42-1December

December
The Taking of Eden, by Robin Alexander, ISBN: 1-933113-53-7

Coming 2006

January
The Illusionist, by Fran Heckrotte, ISBN: 1-933113-31-6

February
Romance for LIFE, Lori L. Lake & Tara Young, Eds, ISBN: 1-933113-59-6,
Private Dancer, by T. J. Vertigo, ISBN: 1-933113-58-8
Define Destiny, by J. M. Dragon, ISBN: 1-933113-56-1

March
Journey's Of Discoveries, by Ellis Paris Ramsay, ISBN: 1-933113-43-X
Assignment Sunrise, by I Christie, ISBN: 1-933113-40-5
Prairie Fire, By LJ Maas, ISBN: 1-933113-47-2
Compensation, by S. Anne Gardner, ISBN: 1-933113-57-X 2006

April
She Waits, by M. K. Sweeney, ISBN: 1-933113-55-3
Meridio's Daughter, By LJ Maas, ISBN: 1-933113-48-0
The Petal of the Rose, by LJ Maas, ISBN: 1-933113-49-9

May
Tumbleweed Fever, By LJ Maas, ISBN: 1-933113-51-0

June
Lilith, by Fran Heckrotte, ISBN: 1-933113-50-2
The Flipside of Desire, by Lynn Ames, ISBN: 1-933113-60-X

November
Times Fell Hand, By LJ Maas, ISBN: 1-933113-52-9